The cold muzzle of a weapon pressed into the side of Adriana's head.

I'm going to die!

"Please." She instantly regretted that she'd uttered a word.

"Adriana?" Brent growled the whisper. "What are you doing out here?"

At the sound of his familiar, welcome voice, she nearly slumped, but he caught her.

"Answer me," he whispered.

"I heard the warning go off. I couldn't let you face the danger alone."

Something foreign flitted over his features, though it was too dark to see his gaze.

"I didn't recognize you geared up like a soldier," he said, and touched her bulletproof vest. In the moonlight, she barely made out a half grin, then it disappeared, his voice laced with weighty emotion. "I...could have killed you."

"I'm grateful you didn't."

"Adriana, I told you to stay in the house, where you would be safer than out here. Why can't you follow my instructions?"

She hated to hear the accusation, the disappointment in his tone. "I couldn't let you face my brother or his henchmen alone. Besides, I'm here now."

And she wasn't leaving his side.

* * *

Texas Ranger Holidays: A Season of Danger

Thanksgiving Protector by Sharon Dunn
Christmas Double Cross by Jodie Bailey
Texas Christmas Defender by Elizabeth Goddard

Elizabeth Goddard is the award-winning author of more than thirty novels and novellas. A 2011 Carol Award winner, she's a double finalist in the 2016 Daphne du Maurier Award for Excellence in Mystery/Suspense, and a 2016 Carol Award finalist. Elizabeth graduated with a computer science degree and worked in high-level software sales before retiring to write full-time.

Visit the Author Profile page at Harlequin.com.

TEXAS CHRISTMAS DEFENDER

ELIZABETH GODDARD

HARLEQUIN® LOVE INSPIRED® SUSPENSE

Special thanks and acknowledgment are given
to Elizabeth Goddard for her contribution
to the Texas Ranger Holidays miniseries.

Recycling programs
for this product may
not exist in your area.

LOVE INSPIRED BOOKS

ISBN-13: 978-0-373-67865-5

Texas Christmas Defender

www.Harlequin.com

Printed in U.S.A.

The name of the Lord is a strong tower;
the righteous run to it and are safe.
–Proverbs 18:10

Dedicated to the One who saved me.
You are my strong tower.

Acknowledgments

As always, I want to thank my amazing writing friends and, in this case, Texas Ranger continuity writing partners Jodie Bailey and Sharon Dunn, for their help and insight in getting it right in this story. You ladies rock! A special thank-you goes to Sherri Tallmon at Hidden Oaks Llama Ranch for her help in answering a few questions about the care and love of llamas. If I didn't already have my hands full I might consider taking on a few of these wonderful creatures! Thanks to Elizabeth Mazer for her encouragement and support and her belief in me as a writer, and to Emily Rodmell for including me in this project. Steve Laube—we celebrate seven years together this year. We've come a long way, Agent Man!

ONE

A hand clamped over her mouth, startling Adriana Garcia and muffling her scream. The muzzle of a gun pressed against her forehead. Her throat constricted.

Though she couldn't see who held the gun to her head, she knew it had to be her drug-lord brother, Rio Garcia, come to extract his revenge.

She couldn't breathe.

The large hands and muscled arms dragged her back and away from Kiana, the pregnant llama she'd been feeding. Adriana dropped the bucket of grain. Kiana stretched her neck, wanting to spit at the intruder. Llamas were excellent "guard dogs" and Kiana had been subtly signaling that something was wrong for several minutes now, but Adriana had misinterpreted her earlier agitation.

Adriana's heart lodged in her throat. Her worst nightmare was unfolding this very moment. Her greatest fear had come true—her brother had found her. He would kill her now.

But not before he obtained the information he needed. Then he would show no mercy.

She should have known it would come to this.

I'm not ready to die. Oh, God, help me! Jesucristo, *save me!*

Even though she'd feared this day would come, and she'd prepared for it in every possible way with the booby traps and a security system, at this moment she realized she hadn't prepared for it in earnest—from the deepest part of her soul.

Adriana had not prepared to die at her brother's hand.

But could she beg for his mercy?

She'd had so many dreams, so many plans after her escape from her home in Juarez and the family drug cartel. Now all of those dreams were turning to dust. Why hadn't she moved much farther away?

It's too late now.

He forced her into the shadows of the barn, his hand still pressed hard against her mouth. The weapon bit into her temple.

"I'm going to remove my hand. Don't scream," he said, keeping his voice low.

His voice…it wasn't Rio, her brother. But no

matter. Rio had sent one of his enforcers…except his trusted lieutenants were all Mexican, and this man hadn't spoken in Spanish. Didn't have an accent.

"Did you hear me? I said, don't scream." He repeated it in Spanish this time, but he was still missing the expected accent.

She nodded. She lost nothing by agreeing. No one would hear her scream except possibly Inez Ramirez, the older woman from whom Adriana leased the llama ranch she someday hoped to own. But this man wouldn't be afraid of Inez.

He slowly lowered his hand from her mouth. The weapon remained aimed at her head as the man carefully stepped around her and into view.

Adriana gasped. Even relaxed a little, because she recognized her captor, and it wasn't Rio or one of his minions.

This man was the Texas Ranger she'd saved two years ago in Mexico. Maybe…maybe today wasn't her day to die, after all. *Thank You,* Jesucristo.

"What…what are you doing here?"

"I'm Texas Ranger Brent McCord, and I'm looking for Adriana Garcia."

"I know who you are." She could never forget the intensity of his green eyes. "And you know who I am, too. Don't you remember me?"

"Are you Adriana Garcia?" He repeated the question, his gaze remaining hard, his tension palpable.

The question stung her as she stared down the muzzle of his handgun. He didn't remember her or what she'd done for him? He'd been a stranger to her when she'd risked her life to save his by distracting one of Rio's high-level henchmen. Or hatchet men, as she thought of them.

The guy would have seen the Ranger and would have killed him without hesitation. Not only had she distracted the goon, but she'd concealed the Ranger in her own home until it was safe to lead him away from the danger.

Her palms slicked, even now, at the memory of the risk to her own life. Her brother had learned of her betrayal only a few months ago, and that had sent her on the run, fleeing to Texas. The truth was she'd wanted an out from their family's horrible, deadly business, though she wasn't personally involved with her brother's cartel. She'd lived in fear for far too long, and helping the Ranger had propelled her on a path to freedom, but she still wasn't completely free. Not yet. Her long-dead American mother would have been relieved Adriana had made it this far out of Rio's grip. That she had even tried.

Had the Ranger known that she'd been forced to run in fear for her life because she'd aided him? He must know something of her circumstances to even be aware that she was in Texas. Apparently he'd been searching for her. Even more disturbing—he'd found her.

She sagged. "You don't remember."

Oh, but she'd forgotten she now wore a disguise—her hair dyed auburn and permed with short curls. Her fake tortoiseshell glasses. She wasn't supposed to look familiar to anyone who could recognize her—that was the whole point. So why had she spoken to him the way she had? Did she *want* him to remember or recognize her?

If he truly didn't know her, then this was her chance. She could deny her true identity. She had to be more than careful. There was a reason she was in disguise, even at the llama ranch. Why, then, did she find herself wanting this man to remember her?

As she studied him closely, the truth became plain in his eyes. This Texas Ranger with the piercing green eyes knew who she was, all right.

She saw something more than just recognition there. *Appreciation?*

Warmth flooded her. She couldn't help but smile on the inside at that. The two of them had a connection from the past. Something about him had drawn her then, and it drew her now, even though he had his weapon aimed point-blank at her.

Right. The gun. She couldn't let herself forget that. She shook off her illusions that the Ranger owed her anything, or that he would never harm her because he felt something for her. He could very well be here on Rio Garcia's cartel business, after all. He could have been bought and turned like so many other supposedly good guys. Everyone had their price.

What is your price, Ranger McCord?

Adriana took a step back. "You know who I am, so why ask the question? Who sent you? My brother?"

"What?" His face morphed into a deep scowl, as if she couldn't have offended him more. "Didn't you hear me? I'm a *Texas Ranger.*"

Though he'd emphasized those last two words, she scoffed. "There are Americans, law enforcement officers, on my brother's payroll. Maybe even *Texas Rangers.* He could have sent you because he knew I would more easily trust you." At his obviously shocked and offended reaction to her words, she almost wished she could take them back. But she reminded herself that she shouldn't trust this man, even if she'd saved him. Even if he owed her his life.

"You mean because you saved me before."

She nodded and noticed that Kiana had shifted around and edged closer, extending her neck.

"You could be a double agent."

His face scrunched up. "What? No...no, I couldn't."

She'd turned the tables on this man. Now he had to defend himself. With his back to Kiana, the Ranger didn't pay any attention to the llama.

"I want to hear you answer the question. Are you Adriana Garcia, sister of Rio Garcia, or not?"

Adriana prayed for direction. And forgiveness. If this man had been sent to kill her, then she'd failed in her biggest mission in life—to take down her brother once and for all. Since her escape from that life, she wanted nothing more than to destroy Rio's cartel. But she'd let her guard down today of all days because it was Christmas.

Christmas...

"Don't you realize it's Christmas Day?" she asked, avoiding answering his question. He already knew who she was anyway. For some reason he wanted to hear it from her. "You're here at my llama ranch on Christmas. Don't you have family?"

He was one serious Ranger to have given up his Christmas for work. Or maybe it wasn't such a sacrifice—maybe he didn't have anyone to spend the holiday with. She understood about being alone, far from her family, on Christmas. The thought both saddened her and filled her with relief that she had escaped that life. Better to be alone than with *her* family.

"If you're Adriana Garcia, you're wanted for the murder of a border patrol agent," he said. "I'm here to take you in. I've heard that you're as ruthless as your drug-lord brother. That you only came across the border to start your own cartel here."

The news rolled over her, crushing her under the weight of it. She was wanted for murder? Her knees buckled and she thought she would drop to the ground, but she stood taller, defying this man's accusations. Her brother must have framed her, somehow. How did she make the Ranger believe her? Words failed her.

If only he understood that the reason she'd had to flee was because she had put herself between her brother and this man, maybe he wouldn't be so willing to accuse her. Though she'd planned to run, wanted to escape her family and break all ties with them for so long, saving the Ranger and subsequently being pursued by the cartel had given her all the reason she'd needed to act.

But for him to accuse her like this…

Did she imagine it or did he aim his weapon a little higher? Did he finger the trigger?

Adriana lifted her chin in defiance. "And what do you believe, Ranger man? Do you think I killed the border agent? That I'm here to start up my own cartel to rival my brother's?"

Agent McCord finally noticed Kiana—llamas were normally friendly and sociable, but the very pregnant llamas were territorial, and Kiana had sensed the danger this man was to Adriana. Though Kiana didn't stand close to him, her ears were back, and Adriana knew what came next.

Did Ranger McCord?

He frowned at the creature and continued to aim his weapon at Adriana. "It doesn't matter what I believe or want to believe. The truth is all that matters."

She released a pent-up breath at that. "I'm glad to hear it. I didn't kill anyone. If it looks like I was involved in the death of a border agent, then I must have been framed by my brother."

Kiana raised her chin and stretched her neck.

"What? What is it doing?" he asked, but did not allow his gun to waver.

"She's letting you know she's not happy with your aggression toward me."

Kiana spit at Ranger McCord from where she stood.

Brent took the spit like a man and didn't move at first, knowing that any reaction on his part could spook the creature into more aggression. Grimacing, he slowly ran his sleeve over his face and swiped at his eyes but kept his weapon trained on this woman—Adriana Garcia.

In the flesh.

But seriously? Could anything smell worse than llama spit? Not even this barn smelled worse.

He'd ignore the llama for the moment. The pregnant animal appeared moody. Adding insult to injury, Brent had come into the barn and agitated her even more, the same as he'd done to Adriana.

But he'd found her, finally found her.

As part of the Ranger reconnaissance team, in Company "E" stationed in El Paso, Texas, his assignments varied, but they'd been on what they'd termed the Garcia Mission for weeks now—trying to capture cartel leader Rio Garcia when he crossed the border in search of his sister. At one point, they'd even learned from undercover operative Texas Ranger Carmen Alvarez the date of a planned crossing. Unfortunately, one of their informants, Valentina, had given them the location but then she'd been murdered. Since then, Garcia hadn't been successful in locating his sister. None of them had.

Until now.

Adriana was the key to Garcia.

As for Carmen…she hadn't been heard from since before Thanksgiving, and they were concerned for her safety. She could either be in deep cover and unable to find a way to get a message out or hiding until she could safely return. At least she'd been able to gather good intel on Garcia. That was how they knew how ferociously Garcia was hunting Adriana.

He wanted revenge for her betrayal and wanted it bad. Because not only had Adriana defected, she'd taken something extremely valuable from her brother—cartel cash and drugs.

The Garcia Mission called for them to find and prevent Garcia from coming across the border and find his sister. And if they found her… They'd been on the fence about whether she should be locked up. Had she come to Texas to start her own cartel with the drugs and money she'd stolen from her brother? Or, as Brent had initially argued, was she a good person simply trying to escape a dangerous situation, needing and deserving their protection from her brother?

Some of the Rangers had seemed willing to consider the second option, at first. But that had changed when border patrol agent Greg Gunn was killed in a sting operation at a salsa factory near the border. All the evidence pointed to Adriana as the killer. Later, they learned that Gunn had been working both sides of the law. *That* news had both stunned and devastated them, but no one more than Ranger Colt Blackthorn, who considered Gunn his best friend. Brent was still sick over it, and Gunn's murder had only increased their unit's determination to find Adriana.

Now all manner of law enforcement was after Rio's sister for the killing. The Texas Rangers had wasted a lot of time on false leads, but Brent… Brent had been the one to find her.

So he couldn't afford to let her get away now.

Except…in his gut he'd believed all along she was innocent. This woman had risked her life to save his in Mexico on a sting gone bad and he couldn't forget that. Maybe he *wanted* to believe she wasn't a murderer. *Wanted* to believe she wasn't working with her brother. But he *needed* to get the truth out of her, here and now.

"I don't want to hurt...what did you say her name was?"

"Kiana."

"Kiana. I don't want to hurt her. Mind calling her off?" Right. Like he would harm the creature under any circumstances. But maybe Adriana wouldn't see through his bluff.

She appeared to consider his words, and maybe even humor flickered in her gaze, but finally it seemed her concern for Kiana outweighed the risk she was willing to take. Adriana lifted her hands. "Let me approach her. I can calm her."

Her English was good. Smooth, like honey, not as broken as he remembered.

"Fine. Don't try anything." *I'm not letting you get away now that I've finally found you.*

He watched Adriana approach the llama, who visibly relaxed as the young woman spoke soothing words.

Adriana's gaze drew back up to hold Brent's.

Good. Now he'd attempt to get the answers he needed. "Why would he frame you?"

Her chuckle was incredulous. "Come on. You're smart. I'm sure you can figure it out."

I have my suspicions, but... "I want to hear it from you."

Adriana dropped onto a bale of hay near Kiana and her shoulders sagged. "My brother is hunting me. There is nothing he wants more than to get his hands on me for what he believes is the worst kind of betrayal." Her brown eyes pierced his.

"Four months ago he learned that I helped you to get away, and I had to escape. And once I was settled, I began enacting my plans to take him down."

Brent slumped under the weight of that news. He hadn't realized how great a risk she had taken in helping him, or that it had been the catalyst to her fleeing to Texas. "Go on."

"So, if he made it look like I killed a border patrol agent, his problem would be solved. Others will find me for him. The Texas Rangers will hunt me down and lead him right to me. And…here you are." Her gaze flicked to the barn entrance.

A chill ran over him. Had he done just that? Led her brother and his bloodthirsty cartel members to this ranch? He didn't think so, because he'd been on his own in his search for her. After the discovery that Greg had been a double agent, they were all wary of sharing their leads through any means that another spy might be able to track. The reconnaissance team didn't know where to find him, which also meant no backup was on the way if Garcia showed up to take Adriana.

Lord, please don't let that be the case.

But her words confirmed his own suspicions as well, that her brother hoped the authorities would lead him to his sister. It had already nearly happened once, when a woman who had borne a surprising resemblance to Adriana had been found by the Rangers—and then subsequently attacked by Garcia's men. That was why he'd been so careful when coming here today. Still, the suspicious tone of her words had him itching to flee the barn and check the perimeter of the ranch.

Her gaze snapped back to him, and her eyes reflected that she noticed his anxiety.

"Look, I didn't lead him here. I came alone." Was he revealing too much? "I had to find you first. On my own."

Emotions he couldn't read shifted behind her gaze and her stern expression softened. "You came alone? But…why?"

He lowered his weapon but kept it ready. "Because I didn't believe you were guilty of murder even though there's evidence that shows you were at the scene."

"What evidence?" Her hands fidgeted.

"A scarf and a bracelet. We've seen you wearing identical ones in surveillance videos." Though Brent had always doubted her ability to strangle a man to death with a scarf—at least, a strong and sturdy man like Greg.

She blew out a breath. "That's convenient, isn't it? I mean, if you're going to frame someone and have access to those sorts of things, makes sense to plant them at the scene, doesn't it?"

His thoughts exactly. He'd said as much to Colt, though his friend hadn't been very willing to listen. "It does. And it also makes sense that if you were there and committed the crime, evidence would be found."

"It doesn't make sense that I would leave that kind of evidence. That's much too obvious."

Hands shaking, Adriana rose from the bale. She appeared nervous, definitely nervous. Brent didn't take his eyes from her in case he had it all wrong about her and she tried something. That possibility remained.

"I left those items behind in my home in Mexico when I fled. Your surveillance videos are from before I ran, aren't they?"

She had him there. But he still had a lot of questions. "What about the money and drugs? Where are they?"

"So you're still unsure of my innocence."

"Something like that." Either she was guilty, or she was in trouble and needed protection. Before he could do anything else, he needed to know which was true.

Though she remained wary of him, she grabbed the bucket she'd dropped. Some of the grain had spilled on the ground, but she continued feeding Kiana with what was left in the bucket.

She drew in a deep breath. "Yes, I took the cash and drugs. That's the biggest reason Rio is hunting me now. Before, he wanted me for my betrayal. There is a penalty for the kind of disloyalty I showed when I saved you. Then he learned about what I'd stolen. A family heirloom. My grandfather's Rolex. In my panic to escape, I thought I might need leverage. Something for which to trade my life, so I took it because it has a removable back that contained a gold key. That key was to the storage unit with the drugs and cash stores."

"And we've seen the storage unit firsthand. Know that it's empty. Where did you hide the goods, and why?"

"After I escaped, I realized I could do more than simply hide. I could take my brother and his cartel down—if he couldn't access all those drugs and cash, the operation of his cartel would be hurt, maybe even collapse. But I had to act fast before he realized I'd taken the Rolex. Before he knew to wait for me at the storage facility. But my plan didn't work. Even though I got away with emptying the storage shed without getting caught, he's still in business."

If she really had believed she could shut her brother down or cripple him by taking one warehouse out of the equation, she could dream on. They wouldn't have been mortally wounded by her actions. But he admired her determination—that was, if what she said was true.

He swiped a hand over his face. Could she be telling the truth? He had to ask all the right questions, cover all the bases. Not let his own gut feelings or his debt to her cloud his judgment. "I would think the right thing to do would have been to turn the drugs and cash over to law enforcement rather than keep them yourself. Keeping them gives the impression that you stole them to start your own cartel."

She gave a cynical laugh. "Right, as if I'd ever consider doing a thing like that. I want no part of that life. I want to be free…" She trailed off, as if she would have said more but hadn't meant to reveal so much, then leaned her forehead against the llama's neck. "You told me that I'm wanted for the murder of a border agent, which proves I cannot trust you. How could I turn the drugs over to you or any law enforcement? Would they let me go? No. They'd keep me locked away. I have to finish my mission first."

"To take down your brother." And then she'd be free, she'd said.

"And I can't do that behind bars, can I?"

"True enough, but you hid the drugs and money before the border patrol agent was murdered."

She held her chin high, anger flashing in her gaze. "I'm Rio Garcia's sister. I couldn't risk turning the supplies over to the law, who would imprison me, one way or another—whether to use me for their own devices or because they would never believe I'm innocent of any involvement in my brother's cartel. I will never give up the drugs and cash. Not until I've taken down my brother. There is no one I can trust. Tell me I'm wrong!"

Brent sagged. *I...can't.*

His grilling her even wore on him. And for some insane reason he couldn't fathom, he found himself wanting her to trust him, as he'd trusted her two years before. "Look, Adriana... I want to believe you."

As she gazed into his eyes, he hoped she read the truth of his words there.

Her face softened and she spread out her palms. "Look, it's Christmas. Inez, the woman I lease this property from, helps me run the ranch, lives with me in the house. We're family now. We had planned our own small celebration. She doesn't have anyone, and apparently neither do you. Why else would you be here on Christmas morning?"

He hadn't taken time off for Christmas in years.

Could he believe that she was innocent and had told him the truth? He'd suspected much of it and had hoped to hear as much from her. But he could very well be blinded to the truth staring him in the face for the simple reason that she'd saved his life before. Any criminal would claim to be innocent.

He wasn't sure if he could trust his own instincts when it came to Adriana. Though he shouldn't, he really shouldn't, he had a soft spot in his heart with her name on it. He buried the thought and focused on his task.

"I haven't decided what I'm going to do with you yet, even though it's Christmas."

A measure of fear flickered in her gaze. "How did you find me?"

"I've been receiving anonymous letters that

gave me clues. Llamas. That you're somewhere on the Rio Grande. The last one urged me to find you before your brother catches you."

She gasped.

"I've visited a lot of ranches along the Rio Grande looking for you, including a llama ranch or two. And I had hoped this would be it. When I saw the booby traps, I guessed it could be you."

"Well, that's comforting, that I'm so easy to locate." She rubbed her arms, clearly distressed. "And then you decided you would just accost me in my barn."

He was a Texas Ranger. A lawman. Why should he be sorry for his actions? But he was. "I had to make sure it was you."

"And you have. My brother won't be long behind you."

"*If* he's tracking me, or has his own lead on you. I only found you because of the letters. Who do you think could have sent them?"

Adriana led Kiana to the barn's exit and urged her outside to the blue skies and sunshine and this beautiful Christmas Day. "I don't know, which is what worries me most. What else can you tell me?"

"We had the letters analyzed. It's someone young. Probably female. We believe English is her second language."

"Rosa…" she whispered.

Who?

Her eyes brightened, lifted to meet his gaze. "It could be Rosa. She was in my brother's cartel. A low-level drug runner. While I wasn't part of his cartel, just being his sister, being Adriana Garcia, made me feel dirty. The only thing I could do to feel better about myself was help people. I figured that God had me there for a reason—to help others get out. Rosa was one of those people. I mentored her and tried to help her change her life. Get out of the ugly business, but…"

"But escaping the cartel isn't so easy," he added.

Brent saw the truth of it in Adriana's eyes— she really wanted to be free of her brother. She wanted to be free of her family ties to the cartel. This young woman she'd mentored was proof enough of that.

"How did she ever know where to find me? I can't believe she sent the letters and has been trying to lead you to me. She must think—"

"That we're the good guys and we can protect you." He cut her off, but he didn't want to risk the conversation taking another direction.

"As long as you, Brent McCord, aren't on my brother's payroll. And even if you're one of the good guys, you still found me and you made it through my security network of booby traps." She paced the barn, agitated. "If you can, so can my brother. He'll be coming for me soon."

TWO

"Tanya!" Inez called, using Adriana's assumed name.

She kept her gaze fixed on the handsome Ranger but angled her head toward the barn door, where Kiana had finally exited. "If I don't tell her something, she's going to come out here to the barn and see you. I don't want her to get hurt."

Adriana didn't see any point in trying to escape the Ranger. He was here now. But she didn't want Inez to come between them and end up becoming collateral damage. Maybe Adriana should have thought about that when she'd chosen to stay with Inez and take on the llama ranch, but Inez had saved her life.

As far as Ranger McCord was concerned, Adriana wasn't sure if she could trust this man yet, though she wanted to, and though she had a strong feeling she could. He tried to appear cold and intense, but she saw the compassion behind his gaze. The problem was that she didn't know if she could trust her own judgment when it came to him—a man she didn't even know. The only thing she knew for sure was that she had saved his life. And risked her own life to do it. That one decision had forever changed everything about her life. Did it matter as much to him as it did to her?

What was it about this handsome Texas Ranger that had her head spinning when she was near him? Had her doing crazy things?

He nodded. "Tell her, then. And don't worry. I have no intentions of hurting anyone."

Sorrow flickered in his gaze. Interesting.

She stepped to the barn door opening. "I'm out here," she called. "I'll be there in a minute, Inez."

Her friend nodded, her bright smile easy to see from the porch of the house. "The cinnamon rolls are baking. They'll be ready soon."

Adriana focused her attention back on Ranger McCord. "Though you say you're not going to hurt us, that doesn't mean I'm ready to trust you. I can't be sure you're one of the good guys. But what now? Are you going to join us for our Christmas celebration or arrest me and take me in?"

He appeared to ponder her question. Hadn't

he already thought this through? Just what had he planned to do once he found her?

Then, finally, he said, "I don't want you running away."

Was that his agreement to spend Christmas Day with them? "Where would I run to? Inez is expecting me any minute. So you'd better make your decision. Are you going to join us, and if so, are you marching into the house as a gun-wielding Texas Ranger?"

He frowned. "I'll…sneak around so she won't see me leaving the barn. Knock on the front door. You can introduce me as an old friend. Act surprised to see me or something."

"Are you saying that you're not going to take me in yet? You're going to let me enjoy my Christmas?" If she even could after Ranger McCord had scared her by holding a gun to her head. Her legs still shook, but she wouldn't let him see her fear.

"If you can still enjoy it while I'm here."

"I'm not going to let you ruin this joyful occasion." Besides, she felt sorry for the man. Anyone who was alone on Christmas deserved her sympathy. "And you're just pathetic enough in your loneliness that I'm compelled to extend a proper invitation to you." She allowed a soft smile for the Ranger she'd thought about for two years, now here with her again. Who would have thought? "Will you join us for Christmas?"

He seemed to consider her request for a moment, questions swirling in his gaze before it softened, his decision made. "I'd be happy to." He stood taller, lingering suspicion in his eyes, but he still offered her a friendly grin and triple dimples lit up his cheeks. She'd almost forgotten about those. Considering the tingling in her toes that they caused, she wished he hadn't flashed them now.

Adriana quickly forced her attention from the attractive lawman wearing a Stetson. "Now, I'll go distract Inez while you sneak out."

"Wait," he said. "I'm letting you walk out of my sight on good faith, because…because it's Christmas."

His tone had softened. *Can I trust you?* She read that desperate question in his eyes and realized he wanted to trust her as much as she wanted to trust him. They were two of a kind—reaching across an invisible barrier that separated them and trying hard to seal their connection.

She nodded. They understood each other. But when she headed for the exit, he tugged her back and gripped her arm, his face mere inches from hers. "I haven't decided if I think you're guilty yet or not. I'm giving you the benefit of the doubt, for now, but if you try anything, you'll soon wish you hadn't."

She didn't like that he'd suddenly tried to sound gruff, but at least she could see his hesitation, see the softer side of him behind the facade. Warmth spread through her. "And if you decide I'm innocent, what then?"

He studied her, his intense eyes taking her all in, unsettling her in ways she couldn't explain. "Either way—guilty or innocent—I'm here to protect you from your brother."

She hadn't asked for his protection. Wasn't sure she wanted it. And for how long would he be hanging around? Adriana didn't like this uncertainty one bit. On the other hand, his presence did add another layer of defense against her brother, should he show up.

Heart pounding, she arched a brow, then yanked her arm free and left the barn. After all Inez had done for her, she wasn't sure she could lie to the woman about her relationship with Brent. Or, rather, nonexistent relationship. Nor did she believe she could hide the fact he was a Texas Ranger who had found her. But telling the truth about Brent would require her to reveal all the secrets that had become her burden to bear in her mission to hide her true identity on the llama ranch.

Inez knew some of it already, of course. Adriana had been here only a month when she'd shared with Inez who she really was. Her old name. After all, Inez had found her dehydrated, bruised and exhausted from the trek across the harsh Mexican terrain until she'd crossed the Rio Grande and collapsed on Inez's property.

As Adriana recovered, thanks to Inez's care, she had known she owed the woman her honesty—to a point. Many secrets had to stay hidden for Inez's own protection, not to mention her peace of mind. One of them having nightmares that never seemed to end was more than enough. So, while Inez was aware of her past, it was something they rarely discussed. Mostly, they focused on the work. The older woman who'd run this llama ranch for years taught her everything in a short time, and Adriana had come to love her like family.

She hadn't wanted to use any of the cartel money but had some money of her own that she'd been stashing away for the inevitable day when she'd have to run. Besides, to purchase the ranch in her own name would give her location away. She and Inez had their own private agreement for now.

She hurried to the house and opened the door, the aroma of cinnamon immediately greeting her. *My favorite.* Somehow she had to compose herself or Inez would read her well enough to see that something had upset her. She absolutely refused to let the Texas Ranger's untimely appearance ruin their Christmas. It was hard enough to celebrate as it was, considering the family she'd left behind and memories of a life when she was much younger, when her mother and grandparents were still alive and before her father had entered his own life of crime, her brother following in his footsteps after their father's death.

She entered the brightly decorated kitchen and breathed in the scent. Normally this would relax her. But not this morning.

Inez instantly looked up from pulling the scrumptious cinnamon rolls from the oven. She set them on the stove and frowned at Adriana. "Tanya, your cheeks are flushed. You're not ill, are you?"

While living here, she went by Tanya Parker and tried to speak mostly English. Yes, Adriana had an American mother, who'd taught her the language, but she had died when Adriana was very young. Died and left Adriana behind to end up being raised in a cartel family.

A second-generation American, Inez had helped her to polish her English and speak it well. With her curly auburn hair and glasses, she might not look or sound like Adriana Garcia, but in the end, she couldn't disguise her Mexican heritage.

Inez set the oven mitts aside and pressed her hand against Adriana's forehead and cheeks like her mother would have. Adriana smiled and stepped away from the woman's reach. "No, it's nothing. Just glad it's Christmas. I look—"

The doorbell rang. Adriana stiffened. She hadn't come up with a story to tell Inez yet. She didn't much feel like keeping anything from her. But how did she explain? "I'll get it."

Adriana made her way to the foyer and peeked through the peephole just to confirm Ranger McCord stood there. Seeing his tall form, his brown hair mussed from the hat he'd removed, his broad shoulders held high, had her heart skipping. His green eyes stared down the peephole and her pulse jumped. The man appeared intense in a way she couldn't help but find attractive.

She couldn't let her emotions run away over him. If only she hadn't been infatuated with him from the moment she'd met him two years ago. Her sentiments aside, she wasn't even sure how she felt about his sudden appearance, even if he promised protection.

Sucking in a breath to regain her composure,

she opened the door and smiled. Somehow she had to get into the act. "What a surprise to see you."

Amusement sparked in his eyes as he returned her smile, flashing those dimples and triggering that tingle in her toes again. She tried to look at anything but his smile, but where? His eyes? His strong jaw? His more than adequate physique? He'd placed his Stetson back on his head and that wrapped up the complete handsome Texas Ranger picture.

She opened the door wide and waved him in with a flourish.

Inez appeared, wiping her hands on a towel.

"This is Brent McCord, Inez," Adriana said, then turned her attention to the Ranger. "What brings you by? You're welcome to spend Christmas Day with us." She hadn't even waited for his answer before inviting him. Adriana hated the way her words sounded so stilted and rehearsed.

She focused her next words on Inez. "That's all right with you, isn't it?"

Inez's eyes widened. Her gaze held Adriana and a small grin lifted her lips as if she knew a secret. "Welcome, welcome, Mr. McCord. If you don't have other plans, we'd be delighted for you to join us. You're just in time for the cinnamon rolls. They're just out of the oven. It's a late breakfast for us. We'll eat our Christmas dinner in a few hours. I hope you like smoked turkey."

The Ranger nodded with a grin. That cute triple-dimpled grin. Adriana wished he wouldn't smile at all, because he was entirely too charming. "No plans at all," he replied. "I appreciate the invitation, ma'am."

Ranger McCord stepped all the way inside and drew in a long breath, the aroma of cinnamon rolls obviously getting to him. Adriana motioned for him to sit on the sofa in the small living room of the ranch house, the huge window in front offering a good view of a portion of the ranch. From that position, they could see the unpaved driveway leading to the house on one side, and a part of the pasture on the other side with llamas grazing in the distance. By the subtle relaxing of his posture, she could tell he appreciated the chance to keep an eye on things and hopefully see any danger that might approach.

Inez returned with coffee and a plate of rolls for them. Adriana watched as the Ranger took a bite of Inez's specialty and closed his eyes, savoring the flavor and texture. When he opened them, they looked right into Adriana's. Unsettling.

She shook off the effect he had on her and grinned. "There's nothing like them, is there?"

"I haven't tasted better."

The shared reaction to Inez's cinnamon rolls oddly broke the awkwardness of the situation, and for a few minutes Adriana believed that she would be able to forget that Ranger Mc-Cord had been searching for and finally found her. And now he would…well, she wasn't really certain what his next step was. At the end of this most holy day, she didn't know what would happen to her. But, for now, they ate and talked as if nothing was out of the ordinary.

"What do you think of my lovely sweater?" Inez modeled it for them. "This was my Christmas gift from Tanya."

Adriana looked at Brent. "We exchanged gifts last night. I guess we were both too anxious to wait to give our gifts today."

"And what did Inez give you?" he asked.

She suddenly felt awkward because they had no gift for him, but he was an unexpected guest. "A beautifully carved leather handbag. I can get it, if you like."

"No need. You can show me later."

"I'm sorry I don't have a gift for you. I didn't know you were coming."

"What?" He twisted his face in mock offense.

"Just a minute." Inez gave a mischievous grin, then disappeared around the corner.

"So what's it like working a llama ranch?" Was this Brent's attempt at small talk? Benign conversation until Inez's return? She'd play along, for lack of any other options. His voice intrigued her—it didn't sound like he'd grown up in Texas. She might ask him about that later, if given the chance.

"I had no idea how much I'd love living and working on a llama ranch." Adriana released a long sigh. "I could live here forever in peace."

Brent moved away from the sofa and sat across from her on the floor, one knee up. His arm rested on his knee. "You mean, if it weren't for the fact your brother is after you," he whispered.

She leaned her head back. "You would have to bring him up. Bad enough you're here, I had hoped to enjoy the day without thoughts of my particular situation." She hadn't forgotten her brother. Would never forget that everyone was after her—including the Texas Rangers—but, for today, she'd needed a reprieve.

"I don't want you to relax. You can't afford to until this is over."

Brent stiffened at the approaching footfalls in the hallway and returned to his previous seat.

Inez held a wrapped package and handed it

to Brent. He frowned as though he wouldn't accept it. Adriana couldn't let him hurt Inez. She grabbed the package for him and handed it over, forcing it into his hands, not letting him refuse. "Merry Christmas."

Pain flickered behind his gaze. What was that about? Reluctantly he took the package. "There was no need," he said as he glanced to Inez. "I'm intruding here, as it is."

"God brought you here today for a reason."

Surprise sprang from his eyes. "Well, I don't have anything to give you in return."

"Of course you do," Inez said. "I know you're here to protect my Tanya."

Brent glanced at the woman. He turned his attention back to Adriana. She saw the question in his eyes. *You told her?*

Adriana gave a subtle shake of her head. Inez was extremely observant and had obviously figured out on her own that things were not as they seemed.

He hesitated another moment, then ripped into the small package. It was a leather-bound devotional filled with God's promises. The leather carving was similar to that of Inez's gift to Adriana, obviously purchased at the same craft shop.

"I had been praying about who to give this gift to," Inez said. "A few moments ago, I knew."

He stared at the gift long and hard before saying anything. For a moment, Adriana feared he would hurt Inez's feelings with his lack of response, but then she realized she knew better. The woman was tough and her faith in God was strong. If she'd felt led to give this gift to Brent, nothing he said or did would make her regret it.

"Thank you." His tone revealed he maintained a tight control over his emotions.

Brent rose to his feet and set the gift on the side table.

Adriana thought at first his action meant that he didn't appreciate Inez's thoughtfulness and was discarding the gift, but then she saw the emotion boiling up in his gaze. He glanced at Inez, true gratitude in his eyes before he shuttered it away.

He unholstered and brandished his weapon, surprising them both. "And now, for my gift, I'm going to check the perimeter. Make good on that promise of protection. Double-check the booby traps. You might want to let me know what and where all of them are so I can find and check them."

"Let this be a test to let us know how well I've hidden them." For a moment, she felt pleased and proud that he needed to ask. But then a dark thought crept in. "Except," she admitted, "you got through some of them before on your own."

He frowned, his thoughts clearly running on the same track as her own. "Right. If it had been anyone else, you'd be dead right now."

Brent had to step away from this situation that had grown far too personal.

"We'll be eating Christmas dinner in a couple of hours. Don't be gone too long," Inez called after him as he shoved through the front door, clomped across the porch and down the steps. He kept his eyes sharply attuned to his surroundings, though his mind remained muddled by the fact he'd found Adriana Garcia and was spending today with her and her friend like they were some kind of happy family.

He never in a million years could have imagined he would be eating Christmas dinner with the sister of drug cartel head Rio Garcia. She'd disguised herself to look nothing at all like the woman who had saved him. And it would have worked, except for those beautiful eyes. All he had to do was look closely and he saw the Adriana he remembered. Her warm brown eyes had been a dead giveaway. Those had been the same eyes that had signaled a warning to him to stay hidden while she'd distracted Garcia's men searching for him. It astounded him to think that, even then, he'd had an instant connection with her and been able to read her easily enough to trust her silent offer of protection.

Then she'd come back for him after leading Garcia's men away. She'd hidden Brent in her own home until she could safely spirit him out of danger. They'd spent that one day together, two years ago. He would never forget that day or those eyes. The hair and glasses might fool others, but up close and personal, they hadn't hidden the luster and compassion in her gaze. At least, not from him.

When he'd seen her before, she'd had long dark hair, but she'd done a great job of disguising it with auburn curls to go with the plain farm clothes that hung loosely off her body. But changing her appearance hadn't diminished her beauty or hidden away her spirited nature. Brent found himself insanely attracted to the woman. Still. After two years. It was why he'd had to be the one to find her.

Her disguise and the fake name, Tanya Parker, had worked well enough that the Texas Rangers and Garcia's cartel had initially gone after the wrong woman—Danielle Segovia, who had been misidentified by a local policeman in El Paso after seeing photos of Adriana. Of course, she had turned out to actually be

Danielle Segovia and not Adriana Garcia. Danielle just happened to be a dead ringer for Adriana, that was, before she'd disguised herself.

The Rangers had received intel that Adriana was hiding in El Paso and running a small crafts shop, Mexican Artifacts and Crafts by Danielle. Though it had seemed odd that she'd attempted no disguise beyond changing her name, they'd thought she was hiding from her cartel brother in plain sight. Ranger Colt Blackthorn, Brent's close friend, had gone undercover to determine if the woman was actually Adriana. But it had turned out she wasn't, and Colt, well, it looked like he had fallen in love. Good for him.

As for himself, attracted to Adriana or not, Brent wasn't relationship material. At least, he kept telling himself that, but Adriana was causing a war between his heart and mind.

Confusion about what his next move should be clouded his thoughts. And he needed to focus in case he'd inadvertently led Garcia and his men to Adriana's llama ranch, as she'd suggested. He couldn't dismiss the possibility when there were lives at risk, even though he didn't think that it was very likely that he'd been followed. No one knew he was coming. Only Colt knew that Brent had gone in search of Adriana, following the clues in the letters he'd received. And even if the whole of their reconnaissance unit had come searching for her, how would Garcia know about it? How could he find out? Was there another mole— someone else, like Greg Gunn, who'd been working both sides?

All this he considered as he carefully made his way to the perimeter of the ranch, vigilant for Adriana's booby traps even as he thought that Garcia's men would know to look for them, as well. In fact, the traps themselves had given the ranch away, confirmed to Brent that he had found the right one. Even though the traps warned the occupants of intruders, they also signaled to others that the property owner was someone who expected trouble.

And this didn't bode well for Adriana.

Regardless of her innocence or guilt, it was his duty to keep her safe. Except Brent knew deep down that his feelings of protectiveness went beyond his duty as a Ranger.

He wanted to believe in her innocence, but he could be misjudging where her loyalties rested. He had a murderer for a father—a man he'd admired his whole life until he learned the truth. His instincts couldn't be trusted. Yeah, Brent could be completely wrong about her. He couldn't let his attraction to her—not to mention his lingering gratitude for the way she'd saved his life before—lead him astray. He had no idea just how much that swayed his judgment, if at all, but he had a feeling it did.

Now that he'd found her, seen her in the flesh again and talked to her in person, seen the passion in her eyes, he realized he'd been thinking about her eyes for the last two years. He'd been thinking about *her* all this time. And he might actually be in trouble here.

He came across an air horn's trip wire and carefully stepped over it, grateful for the distraction. Adriana had tripped the outer booby traps to his heart already—and he reminded himself she was a fugitive. Could be guilty of crimes as heinous as murder. And even if she wasn't guilty of that, she'd certainly stolen drugs and money from her brother and had not turned them over to the authorities. There was a lot she had to answer for—and until he got those answers, he had no business thinking of her in romantic terms. It could mar the Rangers' investigation.

After he'd successfully avoided more of her booby trap alarms and was reassured that no one nefarious lurked near the ranch, his tension eased, if only a little. The cartel drug lord might not be in the near vicinity, but Garcia could very well be on the way. According to Agent Alvarez's intel, the drug lord already

THREE

After savoring the last bite of delectable smoked turkey, corn bread dressing and the other delicious sides prepared with an El Paso flair, Adriana set her fork on her empty plate. She'd eaten entirely too much, but it was Christmas. If they couldn't indulge a little while celebrating the day set aside for the birth of Christ, then what was left? Inez rose and grabbed the dish.

"I'll help you with the dishes." Adriana stood to clear the table, as did Brent.

"I can help," he said.

"No, no, no." Both she and Inez spoke at the same time.

Her fingers brushed his as she took the plates from him, sending a current racing up her arm, and she flinched away from him, not as subtly as she should have, clanking dishes. A knowing look lingered in his gaze. Adriana rushed to the kitchen, hoping he hadn't noticed the sudden current as they touched as well, and her obvious reaction.

Sharing the meal with a Texas Ranger who had hunted her, a stranger for the most part, had been...well...strange. The strangest part was that it should have been awkward, but it wasn't. Instead, it was downright pleasant. They had both managed to put aside their pressing situation and actually enjoy the meal together, enjoy each other's company. For Inez's sake, of course.

Adriana would keep telling herself that.

If only she didn't like so many things about the guy. She liked the sound of the man's laugh. The way his intense green eyes crinkled at the corners and those triple dimples in his cheeks.

And the way he'd said grace over the meal... like he personally knew the One whose birth they celebrated today. That had given her goose bumps. Brent McCord had too many good qualities that she admired.

Stop it. Just stop it!

She absolutely could not let her emotions run wild where he was concerned. But how did she gain control over them? What was it about him that had had her risking her life to save him before? And now, inviting him to share Christmas with her. He was a hunter and she his prey. She should want to get as far away from him as possible rather than feeling an unstoppable attraction that kept pulling her closer.

"You should go spend time with your guest." Inez stuck the dishes in a sink of soapy water. "When did you learn he would come?"

"Oh, I was as surprised to see him as you were."

Adriana dried each dish as Inez handed it over, and she could easily tell by the woman's expression she wasn't fully convinced.

"Inez, how did you know that he was here to protect me?" Especially since that was only one of the reasons he'd come to the ranch. Just how much had Inez already figured out? Did she understand the Ranger could haul Adriana off to incarcerate her at any moment?

"He has the bearing of a protector. It flashes strong and determined in his eyes when he looks at you, as if you are something precious to be carefully guarded." Inez held her gaze, but Adriana had to look away before the woman read too much there.

Inez chuckled and went back to washing dishes. "And he's not just a protector—he's a handsome cowboy with good manners who seems to love God. Add to that the way you look at each other, makes me wonder why you haven't mentioned him before." Inez glanced up from the dishes again, her face wrinkled with her smile.

That Inez could read Adriana so easily wasn't good news. Nor did she want it to be true, what the woman had implied—that there was a clear connection between them that was visible to anyone who cared to look. Could it be that she'd had a crush on him ever since she'd saved him? Some odd emotional connection originating in their brief time together? She didn't want that to be the case, but the way she reacted told her it was true.

Her heart pounded erratically when the image of the first time she had seen him came back to mind as clear as if it had happened yesterday. She had managed to avoid participating in her brother's cartel, but she'd been in the wrong place at the wrong time. Seen a man hiding as gunmen searched. What was she supposed to do? Stand idly by and watch them find and murder him? She would be as guilty as her brother if she stood by and did nothing, so she'd distracted the man who'd come the closest to finding the Ranger and told him she'd seen someone running in the other direction.

After they'd taken off, she'd approached the hiding man. Fear and determination had both shone through the Ranger's gaze, and something had pinged inside her heart. She hated her brother's cartel. Hated the murder and the bloodshed, but there was often nothing she could do about it. That was why she'd wanted to escape. But, in that moment, she'd known she had to do something more—to find a way to sabotage the cartel so that she could bring it down.

The first step would be to save the man hiding from her brother's henchmen. So she'd taken it one step further and hidden him in her vehicle and then in her home until she could safely lead him out and away the next day in the early hours.

"I see you're thinking about him even now." Inez's words pulled her back to the moment, where she stood looking at dirty dishwater instead of gazing into the appreciative Ranger's eyes.

Adriana frowned but let Inez see at least a half smile. "It's not like that between us."

Seeing him again this morning had terrified her, and yet a thrill had run through her at the sight of him. Crazy. Absolutely crazy. She couldn't afford to be drawn to him. Had to pull away to save her heart. Somehow she'd have to keep him at a distance.

If only she could shake the connection with

him, shake how much she liked him. Surely the attraction wouldn't be too difficult to stifle. Yes, he was strong and brave and capable and protective and, as Inez said, a handsome cowboy. But he didn't trust her, so she could use that suspicion to tamp down on those runaway emotions for the Ranger. Nothing strong and lasting could be built on such a shaky foundation.

"I'm sorry, Inez, I haven't... I haven't been completely honest with you. He's a... He's a Texas Ranger."

Inez's eyes grew wide and she studied Adriana but said nothing as she waited for an explanation.

"He came to arrest me. The Texas Rangers believe I killed a border patrol agent."

"Oh." Inez covered her mouth, then slowly dropped her hand. "And this man, the Ranger, he believes you're guilty?"

"I'm not sure if he believes I'm innocent or not. Either way, what he personally believes doesn't really matter. The other Texas Rangers, and probably other law enforcement entities as well, are out there hunting me."

"But Mr. McCord, Ranger McCord, was the one to find you. He seems willing to hear you out—to believe that you're not a killer."

Adriana shrugged. "Even if he is, what can

I say to convince him? I have no proof of my innocence. There's evidence that I was there that night, at the salsa factory on the border."

"Evidence? But what evidence? I know you did not kill this person. I know you could never kill anyone."

Adriana drew the woman into a brief hug, then released her. "Thank you for believing in me, for trusting me even after everything you know. You're the only person who knows the truth about me. You're the only person I've trusted up until this moment."

"Do you mean to say you trust the Ranger?"

"I want to trust him, but if I'm wrong, that mistake could be deadly."

"This murdered man. Tell me about him."

"I don't know much—I didn't even realize I was a suspect until the Ranger told me earlier today." Adriana gave a hesitant laugh. "But I vaguely remember hearing about the murder the next day on the news. I think his name is Greg Gunn and he was found dead at some salsa factory."

"Yes, yes. Border Patrol Agent Greg Gunn!" Inez seemed unusually excited. "I remember hearing about the murder on the news the next morning. That night, I hadn't been able to sleep and had gotten up for a glass of milk. I saw you heading to the barn with a bucket of grain to care for Kiana again around two in the morning. There's no way you could have been committing a murder that night, because you were in the barn taking care of your llama. I waited in the kitchen and drank my milk, in case Kiana decided to go into labor early, since she was having so much trouble already. So, my friend, you have an alibi."

Adriana couldn't believe what Inez was telling her. "Are you serious? Oh, Inez!" She hugged her again. "Thank you, thank you."

She released the woman before she crushed her with gratitude.

"Now," Inez urged, "go tell your Ranger the news."

Adriana hoped that Inez's testimony would be proof enough that Adriana hadn't committed murder. She slipped out of the kitchen and into the dining room, but Ranger McCord wasn't there. Maybe he'd gone to check the perimeter of the property again. The fact that he'd found his way onto her property without setting off any of her booby traps, or that he'd found her at all, served as a warning that others far more nefarious could follow his lead.

She hadn't allowed the full meaning of it to hit her. Until now. The nightmare was closing in on her. Rio would find her soon. She should be grateful for Ranger McCord's appearance—

it was a forewarning that her time of hiding was coming to an end. But she didn't want the Ranger's life to be in harm's way from her brother and his men again.

The most dangerous man alive was hunting her. She'd saved Brent once before, and he might be tough, but she wouldn't endanger his life again. And yet, how exactly was she supposed to get rid of him? Since he'd arrived, he appeared to have every intention of staying close to Adriana one way or another. He wanted to bring her in on the charges against her, as his orders dictated, but she sensed that he truly wanted to protect her from any attacks, as well. Both motives meant he wouldn't be easily sent away.

Regardless, she had to find him and tell him about her alibi so that he would believe her, truly believe that she was innocent. The fact that she wanted to convince him for far different reasons than her imminent arrest disturbed her. She cared more that Brent, the man, believed her than Brent the Ranger.

Adriana opened the door and attempted to step through to go outside at the exact moment that Brent was stepping inside—they remained in the doorway together. She hesitated in moving forward, as did he, which resulted in them standing much too close. Attraction sparked between them and somehow prevented either of them from pressing on. The mistletoe above them caught her attention.

Mistletoe?

Inez!

When had the woman hung that sneaky, obnoxious sprig of scrub brush?

Her heart hammered at the thought of kissing this brave and strong protective Ranger. The masculine scent of his cologne wrapped around her and filled her head. Adriana had thought of him far too much over the two years since she'd met him. They had emotionally connected then, and the sparks between them at this moment proved that neither time nor distance had diminished that connection. But what did she do with it now? She couldn't think straight with him standing so near.

She quickly stepped away, heat warming her cheeks.

The way he looked at her, the longing in his gaze, she couldn't help but wonder—if she'd remained under the mistletoe, would he have kissed her?

Full soft lips. Warm brown eyes and dark eyelashes. Blushing pink cheeks.

Brent's heart bucked like a wild horse.

He had to gain control of himself. Had to

snuff out his overwhelming desire to kiss Adriana—a fugitive being hunted by the Garcia cartel, not to mention the Texas Rangers and law enforcement at large. She'd manage to elude everyone chasing her for weeks now, but there she stood—the woman he'd come to find—and his head was filled with thoughts he shouldn't have about her. What had gotten into him?

The beautiful Adriana Garcia. That's what. The thick emotions swirling in her gaze nearly undid him. She felt entirely too close, even after she stepped away.

Her eyes locked with his and he could easily see the longing that glistened in her gaze. But she shuttered it away and took another step from him. He had no doubt of her attraction to him, but he also understood that she wanted to keep her distance. Funny how the two of them could understand so much, could agree on the invisible boundaries, without uttering a word about it.

Good. Hopefully, between the two of them, they could keep their distance. And focus on staying alive.

She cleared her throat. "What now? Are you going to turn me in to the law? Take me to your Rangers' headquarters?"

Adriana had asked him the question boiling

through his thoughts all day. He shrugged because he wasn't ready to answer yet. He was still biding his time, hoping she would open up and tell him more about the stolen drugs and money and whatever she knew about Gunn's murder.

"Christmas Day will be over soon," she said. "I have some chores to take care of. The llamas don't take holidays."

"I can help with that," he said. "I meant to ask you—when I scouted the ranch, I didn't see any ranch hands around. Did you give the help today off?"

She shook her head. "Inez and I can easily handle thirty llamas without any extra help. With the ranch being so near the border, I've been afraid if I bring on a stranger, a ranch hand, that someone could recognize me. Either someone who works for my brother, or someone from law enforcement."

"What about Inez? You weren't afraid she would recognize you and tell someone?"

"When she found me, she knew nothing about my identity—that I was Rio Garcia's sister—or about those searching for me. But eventually I told her everything. She's my only friend in this."

Brent found himself wanting to be her friend, as well. He wanted to see trust in her eyes when she looked at him. He was too quickly losing his objectivity with her. "I'm sorry you've had nowhere else to turn, and I'm glad you at least have Inez and this ranch." He motioned to the old cracked-leather sofa. "Can we talk?"

She nodded and joined him.

"I think you're right that Garcia will eventually find you. So you need protection, more protection than I can offer on my own. My team can help you, but we need reasons to trust you. You say you didn't kill Greg, but I need proof, Adriana. I want to believe you." He scraped a hand down his face. That wasn't true. "I *do* believe you, but the others I need with me to help me protect you might not be so easy to convince." And was that the whole of it? Brent had been far too easy to convince because he was defenseless against Adriana's warm brown eyes.

"Ranger McCord…"

"Call me Brent, please." Oh, now he was making it personal. But he'd never liked formality anyway.

"Brent." She sat taller, excitement in her eyes. "I have an alibi."

"What? Why didn't you tell me that before?"

"Because I didn't know. I didn't even know I was wanted for murder until you showed up.

I didn't realize I needed an alibi. But I told Inez that there was apparently evidence against me, and she remembered something important. And it's because you came looking for me that Inez even mentioned this to me."

"Go on."

He listened as Adriana explained Inez's story, then he spoke to Inez himself to hear the words from her lips, see the truth in her eyes, verifying the facts. He couldn't believe how much relief swelled inside. Relief that Adriana, this woman who was still hunted by the law, was innocent of murder.

Yes, she admitted she possessed her brother's drugs she'd stolen from the Texas warehouse, but there was no evidence that she'd taken the drugs to establish her own cartel, which was the main concern the Rangers had held. In fact, she claimed her intent was to ruin Garcia's cartel or at least destabilize it. Maybe he was right about what kind of person she was, after all. And the best news was that this confirmed what he'd known in his gut, which meant he could still trust his instincts. Knowing the truth allowed him to make a decision.

He found Adriana in the barn cleaning up the spilled grain.

"Well?" She eyed him.

He saw the hope in her gaze and also not a

little fear. Inez's story was pivotal to proving Adriana's innocence. Brent nodded in reply to her unspoken question—*Do you believe me now?* He'd already told her he believed her, but proving it was the issue. "Inez's words ring true." He released a long, grateful sigh.

"But will the others believe her?"

"Yes. And they'll trust me in this." He hoped. After Greg's death, Colt hadn't been able to see straight for wanting to get his hands on Adriana himself, but in the end, Colt had trusted Brent to find her and had been willing to consider the idea that Brent's intuition about her innocence just might be right—she hadn't killed Greg Gunn. Yes, she was guilty of taking the drugs and money—but as a means to bring her brother down and as a means to survive. It could be used as leverage against her brother. Plus, if they arrested her for the drugs, they might not get what they wanted in the end—her brother, Garcia.

"If you aren't going to arrest me, then what are you going to do?"

"I'll stay here and watch the ranch, protect you while I contact my team, and we'll discuss the best way to keep you safe." He just hoped his team and superior, Major Vance, would see things the same way he did. Their initial mission had been to stop Rio Garcia from coming across the border, but now they wanted to capture and arrest him. They had negotiated with the Mexican government to incarcerate him in the United States, but first they had to catch him. Brent had already failed miserably, letting the man get away in the past when he'd come so close to capturing him. He'd carried the guilt of that failure around with him, but finding Adriana might turn the tide in their favor.

Adriana paled. "It's not necessary, really."

Was she afraid they wouldn't buy the alibi? Or was something else keeping her from accepting his offer of his team's protection? "Of course it's necessary. You can't hope to face him and win on your own. You know as well as I do that he could be on his way here right now. If I found you, then he can find you, too. So I'm staying until we can move you somewhere you'll be safe. End of story." *Or I could have led him to you.*

"End of story? You need to understand that I won't leave the ranch. I won't leave the llamas or pregnant Kiana. I've been perfectly safe here. No one knew where I was until you showed up. So get it through your head, I'm staying right here. I can't run from my brother forever." Her voice trembled with her words of bravado. She hung her head, then lifted her gaze to his. "And, Brent, one more thing. I saved you from my brother once before, but I don't want to have to save you again. So maybe it's better that you let me fend for myself."

"Not a chance." Of course he wouldn't leave her to fend for herself. What was she thinking? He wouldn't leave her regardless. The Texas Rangers weren't finished with her. Even though she hadn't murdered Gunn, there were still unanswered questions about the drugs and money. Like where she'd hidden them. But one thing at a time. Brent chuckled, hoping to bring levity to the somber conversation. He was still monumentally relieved at the news of an alibi. "And I don't think you need to worry that it will come down to you putting yourself in harm's way again to save me." He gave her a half grin. "Give me some credit, will you?"

And was rewarded with a soft smile. "I've never doubted your abilities." Then she suddenly turned shy and stood. "I don't know that anyone in this house is going to sleep tonight, but if you're staying, I might as well show you to the guest room."

"Now it's my turn to say it's not necessary."

She gave a tentative grin. "Maybe not, but Inez will insist that you have your own space. You have to sleep sometime. You can bring your stuff in, if you carry a change of clothes with you."

Brent nodded his acceptance of the offer. "I wouldn't want to offend Inez."

He'd parked his truck outside the entrance to the ranch and hiked in. It was probably about time to retrieve the truck and bring it closer, so he'd do that after Adriana showed him the spare bedroom upstairs.

Later that night, he peered out the open window on the second floor, letting the low-forties temperature cool his room as he watched for trouble. He might even set up some additional warning systems around the ranch, if he had time.

He held his cell phone to his ear, dreading the call he was making. He and Colt were on good terms again now, but they'd had a monster of a rough patch when all the evidence had pointed to Adriana, and only Brent had believed she'd been framed. Their disagreement over Adriana's guilt had nearly destroyed their friendship. Although the guy had said he understood Brent's need to find her on his own, Brent wasn't sure how Colt would react once he heard the news that Adriana truly had been found.

When Colt answered, Brent started in,

"Sorry to bother you on Christmas." *God, please help me. Please let Colt believe me.*

"Hey, buddy, Merry Christmas to you, too. Is everything all right? Or are you just calling to ask about my day?"

Brent drew in a long breath. Colt knew him all too well.

"I found her." His gut churned as he waited for Colt's reply.

Silence met him. Brent held his breath.

Then, finally, Colt's voice came through. "What did you say?"

"You heard me. I found Adriana Garcia."

More silence met him over the connection. "Did you hear me?"

"Where is she?"

"Listen, Colt, before you get any ideas to the contrary, not only did I find her, but I have confirmed that she's innocent of Greg's death."

"You *want* her to be innocent, Brent. You can't believe she would be guilty because she saved you that one time. Don't let that cloud your judgment."

And he was so glad he'd waited to find the proof before he contacted Colt. Otherwise, they might go right back into their heated disagreement all over again.

"She has an alibi."

"What is it?"

Brent explained about Inez.

"She could be lying."

"She's not." *Come on, trust me, man.*

Colt blew out a breath. "So bring her in. We'll question them both here."

Why? Didn't Colt trust his judgment? "That's not a good idea."

"Oh, yeah? Why's that?"

Brent scraped a hand down his face. *Listen to me, Colt.* "It's like I thought. Garcia framed her. He wants us to find her so we can lead him right to her. Gunn might not be the only law enforcement officer who Garcia bribed into working both sides. Bringing her in could put her in more danger." Brent cringed. Had he really just brought Gunn's crimes into this?

Colt hesitated, then said, "What's your plan?"

"She stays at the ranch for now. We can protect her from Garcia here."

"You mean, stake out the ranch and hope he shows up so that we can arrest him here and won't have to extradite him from Mexico."

"No, that's not exactly where I'm coming from in this."

"Figures." Colt's teasing tone came through the cell and Brent relaxed a bit. If Colt was teasing him, that meant he wasn't angry. Maybe this time he really did believe Brent that Adriana wasn't a killer.

"If he shows up, that would be a worst-case scenario," Brent admitted.

"And yet, we want him for the crimes he committed. We want him for Greg Gunn's murder and others. If he shows up there at the ranch, we can take him."

Brent blew out a breath. This wasn't exactly the way he'd wanted the conversation to go, but Colt was right. "Our mission here needs to be centered on protecting Adriana Garcia from her brother. I'm supposed to keep her safe, not use her as bait." Except Brent knew Colt was right, too, had always known Adriana was the key to everything. But he didn't have to like it.

"That's up to Vance. Maybe you should have called him first."

"You know why I called you first."

"Yeah, I do. And I appreciate it, brother. And just for the record, I do believe you about the alibi. I trust your judgment. But you know you'll have to clear all your plans to stay at the ranch through Vance. My guess is that whoever he assigns to protect her while watching for Garcia will take some time to get there. We just got some new intel tonight about where Carmen might be hiding."

Brent's heart jumped at the news. They

needed to find their undercover Ranger and make sure she was okay.

"Some of us will be heading out to follow up on that lead. Until then, it's just you. I'll see if I can get there sooner. Are you good with that? Otherwise, you could just bring her in."

Except Adriana would not leave her llamas, willingly, especially with pregnant Kiana ready to give birth any day now. Brent didn't blame her. "I'm good with that. I can hold out on my own for now."

Unless Garcia showed up with a small army.

FOUR

Two days after Christmas, Ranger Brent Mc-
Cord still made Adriana's breath hitch when
she spotted him in the distance, cowboy hat
and all, checking the perimeter at the back of
the property. But along with the surge of attraction she felt was a shiver of worry about
him—he could easily be picked off by one of
her brother's snipers across the river in Mexico. Yes, she'd watched him donning a body-
armor vest on more than one occasion, which
made her breathe easier. But not too much.

She never would have dreamed a Texas
Ranger would act as her bodyguard, let alone
that the Ranger in question would be Brent
McCord. After she saved his life, she'd doubted
she'd ever see him again, and yet she'd held on
to her private little crush inside—that much
was obvious.

While he checked the perimeter, she would
do some checking of her own. Besides, she

could use the fresh air. She stepped out into the brisk day and pulled her jacket tighter against the cold that made her nose run and her eyes water. Checking on Kiana, she found the llama a good distance away and encouraged her closer to the barn. When it came time for the llama to give birth, Adriana wanted her to calve inside the walls that would protect the *cria* from the elements. And, well…if they were in the barn, then Adriana wouldn't have to be vulnerable and out in the open, either. And wouldn't that just be the worst timing if Rio decided to show up then! She was letting her thoughts run away with her. Still…

God, please let the birth go smoothly. And please let the Texas Rangers get here to help Brent. Let them end this once and for all.

Adriana couldn't imagine what it would feel like to finally be free of any fear of her brother's rage once and for all. The kind of free where thoughts of her imminent demise by his hand didn't constantly linger at the back of her mind. The kind of free that didn't cause her to panic when neighbors knocked on her door. The kind of free that allowed her to go into town and shop without worrying someone would recognize her as Rio's missing sister. She feared he had his spies everywhere searching for her, even in the small Texas border towns. Hence, she went by Tanya, had changed her appearance and, for the most part, avoided interacting with anyone other than Inez.

She couldn't afford even the smallest of mistakes—they could be deadly.

As she spent more time with Brent, one question nagged her. Was he here to not only protect her, but to go the extra mile because he felt he owed her for saving his life? She thought she'd seen something more in his eyes. And, if so, what did it matter? She was crazy to want there to be more between them than a common cause. And through it all she'd had this strange sense that they were two people who stood on opposite sides of a railroad track and were reaching across to hold hands, though a freight train named Rio Garcia was bearing down on them.

Her nerves remained on edge at the possibility of what she might expect in the near future once his Texas Rangers arrived in full force. Or would Rio beat them to it?

Trying to grasp the calm that eluded her, Adriana walked the fence surrounding the pasture where the llamas grazed. Though living on the ranch had brought her a measure of peace after everything she'd been through, maybe that tranquility had existed only in her head to begin with. Her deepest desire and need was to feel safe and secure, and she'd pretended she could have that here on the llama ranch. But now her eyes had been opened to the truth. Nowhere was safe—not as long as her brother remained at large.

Caring for the llamas normally soothed her, but not today. She should be working on halter training for some of the younger llamas in the herd even now, which was her usual schedule, but she couldn't focus. It wasn't fair to the animals, who needed her care and attention no matter the crisis that might be occurring around her, but she couldn't change the way she felt. She was upset, her rhythm thrown off when nothing more had happened than the appearance of a Texas Ranger. Still, that should be enough.

She walked the outer edge of the fenced property and noticed a couple of llamas were thin, despite their thicker winter coats, and made a mental note to add some orchard-grass hay and grain to their feed, like she'd done with the pregnant Kiana, who would give birth any day now. Adriana wanted to call the local veterinarian but feared bringing in strangers. Besides, Inez had reassured her she'd assisted in llama births for many years and had never lost a *cria* or a mother. They would be fine.

The sun warmed Adriana, but a cool winter breeze gusted over her, chilling her to the bone. She let her gaze drop to the ground on the other side of the fence, tugging her jacket closer, and her eyes fell on one of her trigger wires just across the fence line. It wouldn't do to have them inside the pasture because the llamas would trip them. So far, she'd kept the traps nonlethal and nonthreatening—just a warning. But with the very real possibility Rio would soon find her, she wished she could go back and replace every single one of them with something more powerful and totally illegal.

Currently, the wire did nothing more than connect to an air horn alarm, which had been the easiest thing for her to set up. Inez had bundles of fishing line, and all Adriana had had to do was order the rest of the supplies online. Eventually she had hoped to run the trip wire the entire length of the fence, set at the spot where the property line began, a few feet before an intruder could even reach the fence. The wire ran about eight to twelve inches above the ground and blended in with the landscape, so it wasn't particularly visible, unless one knew what to look for. Once tripped, a supporting stick would then drop a rock onto the air horn and it would blast out a warning, possibly also disturbing the llamas, too—another added layer to the warning mechanism.

She followed the wire with her gaze as she walked, remaining on the inside of the fence, searching for the booby trap, and then she found it.

The rock was flat.

She sucked in a breath. She'd told Brent she'd stick close to the house; now she'd ventured to the property line and found the alarm had been triggered or dismantled. Before she let panic set in, she thought through the possibilities.

Perhaps an animal had triggered it—a raccoon or a skunk. Or a llama that had jumped over the fence and then come back in. Or the signal could have malfunctioned. Anger replaced her panic. But she needed to check that trap and see if she needed to buy another air horn. If it had gone off, then why hadn't she heard the sound? She climbed over the fence and crept to the rock. When she lifted it, the air horn was gone.

The air rushed from her lungs.

Heart pounding, she jerked her head up to search the property. No animal had triggered this. Had this occurred after Brent had walked the property, or had he missed seeing it? Or worse…had he purposely disabled it? If so, did that mean he was working for her brother, after all? No, she wouldn't believe it. She couldn't believe it.

Please, Jesucristo, *let it not be true.*

Her breaths came fast. Suddenly realizing just how vulnerable she was, panic well and truly set in. She had to climb back over the fence and find and tell Brent. They could be in clear and present danger. She'd left her cell on the table. Idiot!

She'd climbed halfway over the fence when a voice hissed in Spanish, "Come with me now."

Adriana's knees buckled. She remained perfectly still, trying to decipher from which direction the voice had come. It had to have come from the trees outside the fence, but which direction?

"Did you hear me?" This time, the words came louder. "Do what I say, or I'll kill your Ranger boyfriend."

Brent! Oh, please, Jesucristo, *don't let them have taken him.*

Images of what her brother's cartel did to their enemies accosted her, and her legs threatened to buckle. But she forced herself not to cower so easily. No way could they have taken him—he was too well trained. That time in Mexico he'd come onto their turf, but here, they couldn't so easily take him without his putting up enough of a fight for her to have heard it and been warned.

This henchman wanted her to come with him and was lying about Brent. He rushed from the tree toward her, pointing his weapon straight at her. A scream lodged in her throat. She couldn't speak. Couldn't move.

Fear paralyzed her.

He grabbed her and snatched her from the fence. She hit the ground hard. Pain stabbed through her. The man straddled her, pointing the gun at her head and spewing words she couldn't make out. But one thing she could comprehend—his sneer. He was pleased he'd caught his prize.

In her peripheral vision she witnessed a rock hurtling through the air. It hit the man in the head with a sickening thud.

The man cried out and fell off her. He groaned and tried to regain his footing.

Now! Adriana didn't wait until he recovered. This was her chance to flee. Who had thrown the rock? They remained hidden. She didn't have time to search for them—had to get away or the man would snatch her again. She jumped over the fence, ran along the edge into a copse of trees farther down and lifted the bush that served as camouflage. There she found the hole she'd dug in the ground in case the day came that she needed to hide. That day was now.

She crawled into the hole, then let the cover with the bush drop over her.

When putting in her warning systems, she'd taken the time to create hidey-holes on the property. Places where she could quickly conceal herself in a desperate situation. That she lived like this—with the constant threat of being found by her brother—seemed surreal. That she was actually hiding in one of the holes now, also seemed surreal.

But the man would never find her. Inez thought Adriana had gone overboard, but she knew now that she'd been wise to create the hiding places on the ranch in case such an instance occurred. She could hardly believe she'd needed the hiding spot but was so grateful for it.

With only a little light filtering through, she caught her breath and waited. If only she hadn't left her cell on the table she could call and warn Brent and Inez. Someone had saved her out there—but if it had been Brent or Inez, they would have shown themselves. Even though she apparently had a helper, she couldn't move from this spot until the man had gone, but what if he went to harm the helper, or Brent and Inez?

Despite trying to prepare for every foreseeable situation, she'd never considered this particular set of circumstances—people were potentially in harm's way while she—Adriana Garcia, the reason they were in danger—hid away.

She couldn't stay here.

Just as she crawled from the space, she heard a vehicle speed away in the distance across the border on the other side of the river. As relieved as she was that the man was leaving without hurting anyone, she couldn't repress a shiver of dread. If he was willing to leave, that meant he'd already gotten what he came for.

And that could only mean one thing.

The man was now calling her brother, drug lord Rio Garcia, to tell him he'd found his sister.

FIVE

Through the window, Brent looked for Adriana while he made a call. He'd come back to the house a few moments ago to find she wasn't there. But then he caught sight of Adriana running toward the ranch. The terror on her face sent his heart into his throat. He ended his call. He'd been on hold and couldn't get an answer anyway. He grabbed his weapon and bounded down the stairs, passing Inez on his way.

"What's the matter?" Her eyes grew wide with fear.

"I don't know. Stay here." He burst through the front door, jumped off the porch and ran toward Adriana, his gaze searching the area for any indication of a threat.

"Brent!" she called, anguish in her tone and features.

She ran right into his arms and pressed her face against him. He tucked the gun away and wrapped his arms around her, remaining prepared to use his weapon if necessary. But Adriana was in his arms shivering. Grass and sticks were littered through her hair. He gripped her arms and pushed her from him to look into her face. "What's wrong? What's happened?" Whatever it was had reduced this strong, tough woman to a trembling clump.

"Someone was here." Her voice shook. "He tried to force me to come with him. Threatened to kill you if I didn't."

He jerked his gaze up. Pulled his weapon out again. "Where? Where is he?"

"I ran away and hid, and then I heard him drive off. He'd crossed the river to get to the ranch, then crossed back over. I found a disturbed booby trap. The air horn was gone! Maybe he planned to sneak onto the property later and I stumbled onto him before he got the chance. But it doesn't matter." She started gasping for breath, clearly upset. "You know what this means?"

A cloud of dread settled over him. "He'll likely be informing his boss he's found you."

It meant the Garcia cartel would be here soon. And Brent couldn't protect Adriana, couldn't hold them off on his own. They were days, if not hours, away from a full-on confrontation. There was no telling how many men Garcia would bring, and Brent had no backup. Not good. Not good at all.

"Come on." He grabbed her arm and ushered her forward. "Let's get you back inside." For all the good it would do. "Don't go out there alone again. What were you doing near the property line? I told you to stay close to the house." Well, at least he knew he couldn't trust her again not to go anywhere on her own.

They made the porch, and he glanced around them before stepping inside, where Inez waited to hear the news.

"So how did you escape him?" he asked.

Adriana explained about the threat and that a rock had hit the man. She glanced up at Brent, pausing at her words as if their meaning just now registered with her.

"Who threw the rock?"

She shook her head. "I don't know. I was too scared to care. They were hiding. He had a gun and he came for me as soon as he realized I'd seen the disabled alarm. He grabbed me. Yanked me off the fence line and straddled me. I think he wanted to hurt me, but he'd been instructed to bring me with him alive. I think he was afraid I would make a run, so he decided to threaten me with harm to you. When the rock hit him in the head and he fell off me, I took advantage of that and hid in one of my spots."

He couldn't help himself and grinned, even in these dire circumstances. "You have hiding spots."

"Yes. I've thought of everything, except for one thing. As I sat there waiting, I was worried about you and Inez. I didn't have my phone with me, so I couldn't call and warn you. I decided to come out of hiding at the same moment I heard a vehicle speed away. I looked through the trees and across the river and saw the dust as the vehicle disappeared."

Adriana pressed her face into her hands.

He couldn't stand seeing her like this. She had to be one of the strongest people he knew, given what she'd endured, but everyone had their limits. It looked like she'd reached the end of her rope. He sat next to her and wrapped his arms around her, cherished the feel of her safe and sound in his arms. This could have gone so much worse and it would have been on Brent's watch. He couldn't let anything happen to Adriana.

He caught Inez's approving gaze. The woman noticed a lot, which was probably why Adriana decided not to keep her true identity from Inez. It would have been a losing battle. And he could understand that she felt alone in the world and needed at least one person in whom she could confide. Brent couldn't be more grateful that Inez was a praying woman—Adriana needed all the prayer she could get.

When Adriana lifted her gaze, tears streaked her face and she swiped furiously at them. "How could I have thought I'd have a chance to live here, to hide here, without any danger?"

"You did for a while, Adriana. You did. You needed that time to get centered. And when this is over, who knows? Maybe you'll find that sense of peace and security you long for. But it's definitely not over yet. I'm going to call my boss and let him know what's happened. To get him to speed things up on his end. In the meantime, we'll have to go over the ground rules again. I'll watch over the ranch and protect you, and I hope to have some help with that soon, but I can't do my job if you're not willing to follow my simple instructions."

"I'm sorry…but if I hadn't checked the _____ ____, he _____'d have sneaked onto the _____ ____ ____ own he of an intruder. You've been warned, but seems to me there was another intruder. I need to find out who threw that rock. Besides you and Inez, have you seen anyone near the ranch?"

"No," Inez said.

Adriana shook her head. "Of course not. I would have told you."

He nodded. "All right. I'm going to check the perimeter again. You stay inside."

"But what about the llamas? There are chores to be done."

He looked to Inez. "You've been here for years, right? Will they be okay if Adriana doesn't do her usual chores?"

"Of course," the woman said. "They have a pasture to feed on and they have plenty of water. They are free to come and go to the barn at will. The only concern we have right now is our one llama, Kiana, who will give birth to her *cria* any day now."

He nodded. "Okay, then. I'll go grab her and keep her close in the barn."

Inez shook her head. "There's no need to fed her grain an hou

"Vance here."

"Garcia knows where we are." Brent went on to explain what had happened. "That means Adriana needs more than me to protect her here." Which had been the plan, but Brent grew impatient for the arrival of his Texas Rangers brothers.

"Let's bring her in, then."

"Can't do that. There's a llama going to give birth any day now. She won't leave. There's an older woman who lives here, who is leasing the ranch to Adriana in a private agreement. Neither of them are going to leave. I need some backup here *now*!"

"I agree. And Adriana is our best chance of catching Garcia."

"I want her protected."

"That goes without saying, McCord. The others are coming in after another dead lead on Carmen. You'll have to hold it together until we get there. If you think she's in imminent danger, then you're going to have to leave the llama and get her out of there. We're coming as fast as we can. Now, what about the cash and drugs? Have you discovered their location yet?"

"She's not going to give that information up until we get Garcia or she feels completely safe. One or the other. It's her only leverage against him should he take her. She took it to bring him down, and without that bargaining chip, he'll kill her on sight if he finds out she's given them up to us."

"Keep working to find out."

"Of course."

"We'll be there as soon as we can."

Brent ended the call, grinding his molars. Texas had the lion's share of the United States–Mexico border with 1,254 of the 1,900-mile-long border. Their reconnaissance team tasks were slowed by the sheer size of the setting in which they worked.

It could take the Rangers hours to get here. That meant they would be here on the ranch alone for hours. Brent didn't like it one bit. He'd start working to convince her to leave the ranch. Her and Inez. But then someone would have to watch over the llamas. As he hiked the ranch, he was mindful of the proximity to the Rio Grande and how easy it was to cross over from Mexico at this point. Once it was discovered Adriana was here, at this particular location, there were any number of ways that the Garcia cartel could approach.

Despite the fact she'd run into someone only minutes ago, he hadn't come across anyone lurking around the ranch or on the periphery who could have thrown the rock to distract the henchman. Possibly it had been a stranger passing by for some reason who had protected her. But why wouldn't they have stuck around to make sure she was all right?

He found the disturbed booby trap. He should have thought to bring another air horn. Best to keep the warning system in place. It could still work and was better than nothing. He searched for her hiding spot—she'd left it open and vulnerable, and it was easy to find now. The woman was more than resourceful, but faced with the reality that her brother's men had found her and would come for her soon, she'd almost crumbled under the weight of it.

He made his way back to the house and helped Adriana secure Kiana in the barn and perform other chores. Watching, always watching. He would pull an all-nighter watching over the ranch.

So much for grabbing a shower.

Adriana met him on the porch, concern in her eyes.

Dusk was on them as he clomped up the steps and planned to push right by her. He'd been avoiding telling her his news. She might see the utter fear in his eyes. "Backup is coming. But we're probably on our own tonight."

She pressed her hand against his arm and he hesitated. Then gazed down at her.

"Brent," she whispered. Turmoil infused her big brown eyes and turned his heart inside out. *Oh, don't do that. Please don't do that.* He cleared his throat. "What is it?"

"I don't want you to get hurt because of me."

That gave him pause, but he held the door open. "You should get inside and stay inside, like I asked."

"Did you hear me?" She slid past him—almost, that was. She didn't go all the way but stood in the doorway close to him and looked up. In her eyes, he saw that she'd turned this personal when he thought they'd had an unspoken agreement to keep their distance.

"I heard you. But you shouldn't worry about me. This is part of my job."

Hurt flickered in her gaze and she moved inside.

"Bolt the doors behind me," he said.

"Wait. What?"

He closed it, hoping she'd stay inside and follow his instructions.

Brent couldn't very well keep watch over the property inside his room. He'd found a few places he could stay hidden while he watched and made his way over to a nearby cluster of trees. Darkness had settled in. He had all his ammo and prayed to God it wouldn't come to a gun battle tonight.

But hours later, the sound of an air horn resounded, breaking the silence. His heart jumped into his throat. One of Adriana's booby traps had just been set off. Fear for Adriana and Inez curdled in his stomach.

Adriana bolted up in her bed and found her heart pounding as she gasped for breath. What had startled her?

She glanced at the clock. It was two in the morning. She'd finally fallen asleep. She hadn't thought she'd be able to, knowing that Brent was out there. It wasn't the kind of situation where she would sleep easier knowing someone was standing guard. No. She worried too much for his safety. Brent was outside, waiting and watching, and if danger showed up, he would face impossible odds.

She scraped the hair from her face and drew in a few calming breaths until her heart rate finally slowed. The air horn. That was what had woken her. But someone had silenced it. With that thought, the fog of sleep cleared and Adriana pushed herself into action. She scrambled out of bed and found Inez standing in the hallway, her eyes wide.

"Go, Inez. Go get in our hiding place." Inez

nodded and grabbed Adriana's hand to pull her along.

But Adriana tugged her hand back. "No, I'm not going."

"But you must," the woman pleaded. "That has always been our plan. To hide in the tunnel and escape when it's safe!"

Adriana hated hearing the desperation in the older woman's voice. Poor Inez. The woman had cared for her. Nursed her back to health after Adriana had collapsed on her ranch, and this was how Adriana repaid her?

"Sweet friend, that was the plan before Brent McCord arrived. I can't... I can't hide in the tunnel knowing he's out there and could need help. The other Rangers aren't here yet to help him. Now go! If you don't, you'll distract me because I'll be worried about you."

Inez hesitated, then finally nodded.

Adriana couldn't wait anymore but had to trust that Inez would do as she'd asked. She left the woman in the hallway, rushed to her gun locker at the back of her closet and pulled out two guns and a knife. She grabbed her body armor and donned a helmet. Sure, she'd had the warnings in place. The hiding places prepared. Enough ammo for a small army. But she'd hoped and prayed it would never come to this.

And now that it had?

Terror raced through her veins.

But Brent was out there. She wouldn't let him go through this alone. After she quickly prepared herself for battle as if she were a highly skilled soldier, she sneaked out of a trapdoor in a shadowed corner of the house and stealthily made her way in the direction from where the air horn had sounded. At least, where she thought it had come from. It was hard to tell because she'd been asleep and startled awake.

The temperature had dropped below forty, but hiking kept her limbs warm and sweat trickled down her back. Halfway across the field, she stopped and crouched low to the ground. Waited and listened.

Had the man who'd tried to take her earlier today come back for her? Had he brought others with him—maybe including her brother?

Brent remained her biggest concern right now as she searched the llama ranch. Unfortunately, the moon was full, and she would be easily spotted if someone was looking in the right direction, even though she crouched close to the ground.

Tonight, just before he'd demanded she lock herself in, he'd put a cold emotional barrier between them. It had been so abrupt, so palpable, it might as well have been physical, and in a way, with the bolting of the door, it had been. But in this moment, she shouldn't be thinking about where their emotional connection stood. It didn't mean she'd leave him out here alone to fight for her—whether it was his job or something more. She never wanted him to be in the line of fire again, especially for her.

"Brent," she whispered.

Movement in the distance drew her attention. She dropped completely to lie flat on the ground and let her gaze roam the area. She saw no one, but had someone seen her? Though the moon shone bright, she tugged on her night-vision goggles, struggling to believe she needed to use them.

A noise from a nearby patch of scrub brush caused her to still. She slowly crept forward until she reached a tree, then stood behind the trunk, her weapon at the ready.

What am I doing? No matter how much she'd prepared, she wasn't cut out for this kind of tension and strain. She'd never been in a gun battle before. Still, losing her courage now meant she could die.

Waiting behind the tree, she listened and watched. *Where are you, Brent?*

She wanted to call out to him. That he hadn't appeared, hadn't found her yet, scared her. He should catch anyone out prowling around while searching for who or what set off the alarm, including her.

The cold muzzle of a weapon pressed into the side of her head.

Oh, God, I'm going to die!

"Please." She instantly regretted that she'd uttered a word.

"Adriana?" Brent growled the whisper. "What are you doing out here?"

At the sound of his familiar, welcome voice, she nearly slumped, but he caught her, kept her from sliding all the way down the tree.

"Answer me," he demanded.

"I heard the warning go off. I couldn't let you face the danger alone." Her heart palpitated at his nearness in the shadows.

"I didn't recognize you geared up like a soldier. And body armor?" He touched her vest. In the moonlight, she barely made out a half grin, then it disappeared and his voice turned somber, laced with weighty emotion. "I…could have killed you."

"I'm grateful you didn't."

"I told you to stay in the house, where you would be safer than out here. Why can't you follow my instructions?"

She hated to hear the accusation, the disappointment in his tone. "I couldn't let you face

Rio alone. Besides, I'm here now. We can talk about this later. How many are there?"

"What?"

"Who set off the trap? Have you caught anyone? And how many did you find?" She caught herself—too many questions.

That half grin again. So he thought she was funny? "Just one so far," he answered.

Oh. He meant her. "Earlier, I saw movement in that direction."

"Let's go, then."

She stayed behind Brent as he tracked low to the ground in search of their intruder. The whole scenario seemed surreal, but she couldn't dwell on that right now and focused on their search. She wasn't sure whether or not she hoped they would find anyone. She didn't want a confrontation. Still, someone had been there. Someone had triggered that alarm. And fear would keep hanging over their heads until they found the person responsible.

When she'd set them up, she couldn't have known how it would feel to hear the alarm and the subsequent need to respond. To march across her property armed and in body armor, ready for a fight to the death. At least she'd prepared—collecting everything she would need—in case she needed to take that kind of action. But for a few weeks, maybe months, she'd been content to live in her delusion of a safe haven.

God, please let us find only one person out there. Maybe the man after her today had nothing at all to do with her brother's cartel, but Rio would come back for her nonetheless. Anything else would be hoping for too much.

"Brent," she whispered. "What if…"

He paused and stepped back to her. Stooped to lean his head closer. "We really shouldn't talk. That could get somebody killed. I don't feel like dying tonight. How about you?"

She shook her head—no, she didn't want to die tonight, either, and she definitely didn't want to get him killed—and followed him. He'd stopped crouching now and walked tall and confident, as if he had no fear. She didn't feel his confidence but kept close to his solid form.

Suddenly he turned and pulled her close. "Get low on the ground and wait for my signal."

"What? No."

"I'm here to protect you, Adriana. Why do you fight me on this? Please, do as I ask or someone is going to get hurt."

The painful desperation was a powerful force behind his words, so she dropped to the ground and let him go. She had never seen this side of the man, even when she'd saved his life and helped him to escape. She shut her eyes, only for a moment, and images of that time flashed in her mind. She'd assisted him in getting away from the area where Rio's men were searching for him, and the next day he'd hidden in her car while she drove him to safety. Just before he fled across the border to meet up with his team, he'd pulled her close to thank her. He'd been so near she could smell the masculine scent of him.

She'd known then that she'd made the right decision to risk everything to protect him, and for a moment, she'd wanted more time with him, wondering what it would feel like to be in this man's arms, this powerful hero's arms, for something more than simple gratitude. To be loved and cherished by someone who fought for good in the world, rather than being linked to someone who spread insidious fear and death everywhere he went.

Then Brent had asked her if she would be all right. He'd been worried about *her* safety. Even offered to take her with him.

Crazy. The man had been crazy to make such an offer. And she'd been even crazier not to take it. And, God help her, she'd wanted to go with him. She had reassured him she would be fine, but that turned out to be untrue. It had taken more than a year, but eventually Rio had discovered her betrayal and demanded her life in forfeit.

Now, to find herself here with Brent, seeing this side of him, sent her senses, her emotions reeling.

A shout broke the silent night. Adriana shot from her hiding place and ran toward the sound.

SIX

Brent snatched up the scrawny guy and held his weapon to the man's head. Were there others, and if so, how many?

But wait. Confusion rolled through him as he took a closer look at his captive. "Who are you?"

"I... I'm sorry." She held her hands up in front of her face as though she expected him to strike her.

She.

It was a woman. Garcia's lieutenants were all male. But there were women in the cartel he could use and manipulate as he pleased. And her presence here could be a trick. "Are you alone?"

"Yes, I..."

Could he believe her, someone who'd sneaked onto the property? "I'll ask again. Who are you?"

"My name is—"

"Rosa?" Adriana shoved past him from behind.

Her sudden appearance startled and angered him. Not so much at Adriana for not doing as he'd asked and staying put, but that she'd been able to sneak up on him. He paused a few seconds to take in their surroundings again to make sure this wasn't a trap and that they were indeed alone.

She hugged Rosa to her, then released her, gripping her arms. "What are you doing here?"

Before Rosa could answer, Adriana turned her attention to Brent. "This is Rosa Morales, the young woman I told you about whom I mentored."

"Are you the one?" he asked, unwilling to divulge any additional information. Let her tell him what he needed to hear.

"And what is your name, please?"

"I'm Texas Ranger Brent McCord."

Rosa nodded. "If you're asking if I sent you the letters, then the answer is yes. My English isn't so good. But I see you found her, just as I have."

He wouldn't be relieved just yet. "This isn't some kind of trick, is it?" Why he thought she'd tell him the truth if it was, he didn't know. But maybe it was more that he hoped, and he needed to ask the question.

She vehemently shook her head. "No, please

believe me. I only wanted to help by sending those letters. I'm here now, on my own. No one followed me."

He had no choice but to believe her. For now. Besides, if she'd wanted to lead Garcia to his sister, she would have sent the letters to Rio instead of Brent. "Ladies, I say we take this gathering back to the house."

Once inside, Brent paced and watched out the windows. Exhaustion threatened his reflexes and mental acuity, but he would watch over Adriana and her friends until his buddies arrived. Then, and only then, would he consider getting any rest. He wished the llama would give birth already so Adriana would be satisfied all was well, and then he could take her somewhere safe.

Inside the house, he noticed that the young Rosa appeared somewhat malnourished. Though it was now after three in the morning, Adriana placed home-baked bread and a warm bowl of stew in front of her. Rosa ate like she hadn't eaten well in far too long. While she wolfed down the food, Adriana suddenly remembered Inez and brought her out from a hidden tunnel she hadn't told Brent about. Interesting. Nor had she told him about her supply of weapons and ammo.

He'd been impressed when he'd realized

it was Adriana who was armed for bear and dressed in tactical gear. Impressed and horrified at how close he'd come to taking her down, thinking she was a dangerous intruder. She wore it well, but though she'd acquired a tough veneer through her life experience, a softness in her expression remained behind her gaze. To his way of thinking, it took a special person to protect and keep that softer side after the horrors she'd witnessed.

Maybe Brent was the only one who could see it, which could be a good thing. Otherwise, that would be a dead giveaway to others she might encounter, and if faced with a battle, she wouldn't come across as someone to fear. Unlike her brother, she wasn't willing to torture or kill.

Thank You, Lord. Thank You that we haven't had to face Garcia and his men tonight. And please let my Ranger brothers get here in time to protect these people.

Brent was contemplating moving Inez, Adriana and now Rosa, even against their wills, if his team didn't show up in the next few hours. Maybe sooner. The risk was too great to continue using Adriana as a lure for the criminal kingpin. Sure, they wanted to get their hands on Garcia. But at what price? Sacrificing Adriana was one that Brent wasn't willing to pay.

"Tell me everything, Rosa." Adriana pulled up a chair, as did Inez. "How did you know where to find me? I think my brother knows where I am now. Do you know anything about when he's coming?"

Brent wasn't sure how Rosa would find a chance to answer the way she was scarfing down the food as if ravenous. Her mouth full, she shook her head, then between chewing and swallowing she told her story.

She began in broken English for Inez or Brent's benefit, but when he told her that both he and Inez were fluent in Spanish, she switched to her native tongue. "I didn't know for sure. I thought back to things you said to me before. I knew you loved llamas. I once asked you if you could leave, where would you go. I remember that distant look in your eyes when you said you could never go too far away from your home because you were anchored there, but maybe across the border. You laughed then, but I thought... I thought you would have gone to a llama ranch close to Mexico if you could."

Adriana cupped her hands over her mouth. A tear rolled down her cheek. *"Gracias Jesucristo,"* she said, before returning her attention to Rosa. "I can't believe you found me. I barely made it to safety, as it was, and to make it to a

llama ranch, especially one with a wonderful caretaker like Inez, I can only give thanks to God. And I am also grateful to God that you listened, took to heart my words." She glanced Brent's way, her eyes locking with his. "And you helped Brent… Ranger McCord to find me."

Her words made him realize he'd yet to hear the full story of her escape. He'd have to ask her later.

Rosa shrugged. "It was all I had to go on. You had mentioned him to me—said that you trusted him. I knew that you would need protection. I didn't know what else to do."

"Thank you, Rosa," Brent said. "I appreciate your help. I might never have found her otherwise, but what of her brother? Maybe she mentioned her love for llamas to Garcia, too." Regardless, after someone tried to take her yesterday, they could be pretty sure Garcia had located his sister. But Brent wanted to hear if Rosa knew something more.

She sagged and pushed her empty bowl away. Inez took it and filled it again, warming the stew in the microwave.

"I don't know if he has any idea where to look for you. I escaped weeks ago. Sent the letters when I had the chance. I've been hiding and living in the woods on my own since then.

They're hunting me now, too, though. When skirting the towns in search of food, I've seen his men and heard them asking if anyone had seen me, so I knew I had to stick to the woods completely. I'm not nearly as important to them as you. I promise I didn't lead anyone here, but I had to go away from the cartel. You taught me so much—made me realize how wrong it was—and I wanted to escape. Plus, if I had stayed, they would have tried to make me tell them where you were. Where I thought you would go and hide. They knew you had been helping me. It wasn't a secret anymore after you left. Rio questioned everyone. It came out that you had been mentoring others to help them get out of that life and live for good. I… I couldn't stay."

Adriana rose, moved around the table and hugged Rosa again. "Well, no more running for you. You found a home here with us. With me and Inez."

Brent frowned. Was that even a good idea considering how close the cartel was to coming down on their heads here? He cleared his throat.

When Adriana glanced at him, she nodded. She understood what he was thinking, he hoped. "At least until I can figure out where you can go to be safe. I'm afraid the ranch is no longer a safe place. One of Garcia's hench-men found me here—"

"I know," Rosa said. "It was Gregario. I threw a rock at him."

"That was *you*?" Brent asked.

She nodded.

"Why didn't you show yourself earlier?" Adriana asked.

Shivering, Rosa wrapped her hands around the newly warmed bowl of stew Inez offered. "I was scared. I had to be sure it was safe here. And I'd seen him on the ranch." She gestured at Brent. "A Texas Ranger. I wasn't sure I could trust him. He could send me back across the border, even though I sent the letters. Was it Brent McCord, the one to whom I'd addressed them? I couldn't be sure."

"There's no need to worry about you get-ting sent back right now. You're a material witness and in my custody for the moment." Brent winked, hoping that would disarm Rosa. Both Rosa and Adriana were witnesses to Gar-cia's crimes. As far as Brent was concerned, the Texas Rangers needed to keep them close. And safe.

With the possibility of Garcia's cartel de-scending on them at any minute, the llama ranch no longer looked like an option for Adriana, and she wasn't going to like Brent's solution. The distinct sound of vehicles approaching drew his attention—at this time of the morning it wasn't the neighbors.

He readied his weapon.

Adriana ushered Inez and Rosa to the tunnel, then ran back to find Brent standing at the window, peering out without disturbing the curtains too much.

"Stay back," he said.

She remained behind him, wishing she hadn't removed her body armor. This might be the day they'd all waited for. The day they'd all dreaded. She held her breath until Brent's shoulders dropped and he lowered his gun.

"It's my backup." He tossed her a glance. A relieved grin spread across his face as he rushed out the front door, letting the colder night air rush in.

She almost followed him out but remembered these men were the Texas Rangers who had been hunting her. Yes, Brent was one of them, but she had an understanding with him. A connection. She believed that he genuinely wanted for her to be safe and for her brother to go to jail. She wasn't yet sure she could trust the others in their group the way she could trust Brent. There had been a traitor within the law enforcement ranks before—Greg Gunn, the man she'd supposedly killed.

Adriana wasn't sure she could share Brent's relief at their arrival. Still, whether there was a traitor among them or not really didn't matter anymore. Rio knew where she was already, now that Gregario had found her. How long had he been combing the area in search of her? She'd been foolish to think she could remain so close to the border.

She pressed her back against the wall and drew in a long breath. Her quiet, safe haven at the llama ranch hadn't lasted nearly long enough. In truth, she'd known it wouldn't last. That was why she had prepared for the day Rio would find her, even while she hoped it wouldn't happen. But she hadn't considered the Texas Rangers would find her first. And now that they had, it was all happening too fast for her liking. She'd have to adapt. No sense in avoiding the inevitable. She was about to face Brent's Ranger brothers, whether she liked it or not.

Opening the door to go outside and face the Texas Rangers, she found them clomping up the steps to the porch—seven men wearing cowboy hats. Brent's fist was in midair, to knock as if he didn't come and go freely here. Feeling overwhelmed, Adriana took a step back, deeper into the house.

Brent acted quickly to encourage her out the door and onto the porch, into the cold night air.

She reached back to flip on the porch light, but he caught her wrist and shook his head. "Just in case someone is watching. The moon gives us enough light for now."

He introduced her to Austin Rivers, Colt Blackthorn, Trevor Street, Christopher Rook, Ethan Hilliard and Ford Morrow. They all eyed her with not a little curiosity.

Adriana didn't know what to do or say next. "Come in." She swung the door wide.

"If you'll excuse us, ma'am, we have work to do." The tall blond guy—Trevor, if she remembered correctly—tipped his hat to her.

She nodded, noting that two of the Rangers remained on the porch and another two went marching off onto the property, their breath puffing out white clouds. Were there more of them already out there? Others she hadn't been introduced to? Her nerves teetered on the edge. *Hold it together, just a little longer.* Jesucristo, *see me through.*

The remaining Rangers—just three—crowded into her small living room, making it feel even smaller, and removed their cowboy hats.

Brent ushered her to the sofa and sat next to

her, but not too close. Her hands trembled and he took one of her moist palms in his bigger, calloused hand, then squeezed, reassuring her. It felt too good, too comforting. She wanted to snatch her hand back. She didn't want to appear so needy and unsure of herself. She'd survived this long without anyone's help—well, except for Inez's.

"Ma'am," Blackthorn said. "Don't you worry. We're going to keep you safe from your brother. You're in our protective custody now."

It sounded strange, hearing a Ranger call her *ma'am*. Hadn't they considered her a murdering, conniving extension of cartel leader Rio Garcia? How could he be that kind? Maybe his manners didn't let him show the disgust he truly felt for her. Still, at *protective custody* she bristled and sat taller. Glanced at Brent.

He squeezed her hand again. "It's all right. Nothing to be worried about."

Brent had already mentioned the custody term when talking to Rosa, but it hadn't sounded nearly as official and terrifying coming from him. She still wasn't sure she liked it. Couldn't they just protect her and take out her brother without putting her in their custody, even if it was "protective"?

She looked back to Blackthorn, searching the man's hard gaze, and couldn't help but wonder if he actually wanted to arrest her instead of protecting her. Brent hadn't believed she'd killed anyone, she thought, even before she had an alibi. He hadn't believed that she'd come to Texas to start up her own cartel, either. What did this man—whom Brent appeared close to—really think of her? More important, why should she care?

After the introductions, she remembered her friends who were hiding in the tunnel and rose, letting go of Brent's hand. The distraction would give her a chance to regain her composure. The Texas Rangers were here in her living room and on her ranch. Adriana wasn't sure what this would mean for her in the long run, but she sensed that her life was about to change forever. Again. For the better or worse she couldn't say.

"Inez and Rosa are still hiding. I should go let them know we're not under attack here."

Blackthorn nodded. "Good idea. We need to have a confab and will head back outside for that."

He glanced at Brent for his agreement and got it. "Give me a second."

The men exited the room, except for Brent. "Now's your chance to get some rest," he said. "You don't need to worry for your safety, at least for the moment." When he grinned, his eyes conveyed the truth behind those words, along with a measure of doubt.

He wasn't one hundred percent certain they could keep her safe. She didn't blame him for that—she'd never believed they could. "I'll set Rosa up in an extra room, but what about the Rangers?"

He scrunched his face. "Adriana, you aren't required to board the Rangers. We'll be fine. And once we've talked strategy, I'm going to get some rest, too."

After getting Rosa settled, Adriana returned to her room. She glanced out the window and spotted two of the Rangers talking—Colt Blackthorn and Brent. By their demeanor she could tell their discussion was heated, and that should have given her cause to worry, but she was too exhausted to care.

It had been years since she had trusted anyone completely with her safety, but she found herself wanting to trust Brent. She *needed* someone. She trusted Inez, but at the same time she felt protective of the woman. Inez wasn't in a position to protect Adriana in a physical way—to keep her safe from Rio. Could she trust Brent?

"Adriana," a voice whispered.

She stirred, panic engulfing her. She sat up and reached for her weapon.

"It's okay," Brent said. "It's me."

"What…what are you doing in my room? What's happened?"

"Your llama is giving birth."

She rubbed her eyes. "Kiana?" She started to throw the covers off, then thought better of it. "Okay, thanks. Could you wake Inez up for me?"

"Already done. She sent me to wake you."

That Inez had sent Brent to wake her instead of coming herself surprised Adriana, but she didn't have time to think more about it.

Brent left her alone. She dressed and made her way to the barn, where she found Inez with Rosa. It wasn't as if llamas couldn't give birth without their assistance, but Inez had determined the *cria* was breech, which could be a problem for Kiana.

Adriana thought perhaps they would need to call a vet, but Inez continued to reassure her that she'd assisted in dystocia—when the *cria* is in a bad position—many times before. And tonight she would teach Adriana and Rosa what she knew. Together they assisted Kiana in a painful delivery, but finally the beautiful *cria*—the baby llama—stood on its own, a sign it was healthy. It rooted and nursed immediately.

Inez, Rosa and Adriana shared a smile.

Adriana glanced at the barn door, where Brent stood with a wide stance, crossed arms and a huge grin. She had the urge to run to him and hug him but stifled it.

"And now, for a name. What do you think, Tanya?" Inez asked, still using Adriana's fake name even around all those who knew her true identity. Tanya was who Adriana had chosen to be on this ranch, and Inez was choosing to respect that—to allow her to define herself, rather than seeing her as an extension of her criminal brother.

"I think that Rosa should name her."

The young Mexican woman with her long, silky black hair and huge brown eyes smiled, but deep sadness filled her eyes. "Maria." Her brow furrowed. "For my mother. I left her behind in Mexico."

Pain laced her words and Adriana drew Rosa to her and held her tightly. If her brother chose to take things that far, Rosa's escape and betrayal could cost the life of her mother— even her entire family. Adriana couldn't help but think Rosa's mother would willingly give her life if it meant Rosa would be free. Adriana would do the same for her own child, if she had one. But that was a price that no mother should have to pay.

She had to stop her brother, take him down

before he had the chance to continue to control people's lives, to murder them if they chose to defy him. She'd known all along that if she were to flee he would hunt her down, and so she wanted to do some damage when she ran. So she'd taken that watch and removed the contents of the storage—and unfortunately, her actions had put more lives in danger.

Adriana had wanted to save lives, not endanger them.

SEVEN

In the middle of this winter night, halfway between Christmas and New Year's, Brent walked with Colt, keeping near to the house and the barn. They'd strategized with the other Rangers about the location of various booby traps and what had happened so far. Discussed yet another failed attempt to find Ranger Carmen Alvarez. The lead they'd followed had come from Trevor, who'd infiltrated the cartel as a low-level drug runner. While the news had seemed promising at first, it turned out to be a dead end. Trevor had come back with them to regroup.

God, please let us find her.

Would he have found himself in the same position as Carmen—trying to hide and escape the cartel, alone with no access to backup—if Adriana hadn't helped him out? He prayed that God would send someone to help Carmen find her way to safety. He hated the deep ache in his gut. They were a team, and finding her was a priority. Protecting Adriana and taking her brother down were also priorities. They were being torn in too many directions, if you asked him. But all of it was tied together.

Wait and watch and protect Adriana, and Garcia should come right to them. The Rangers were on high alert at the ranch—at least half of the reconnaissance team was here.

Having his brothers with him to watch his back and share the responsibilities was a massive load off Brent's mind. But it didn't make all of his worries disappear. Nothing could change the fact that they were in for a hard battle. And that was why Brent needed to talk to Colt alone. Speak his mind and not hold anything back.

That was something he'd always been able to do with Colt—at least, until a few weeks ago when Greg Gunn had been killed, and he and Colt had disagreed about whether or not Adriana had been involved. But they knew the truth now, and Colt had said he trusted Brent, believed him when he said that Adriana was innocent. That surprised Brent more than a little, considering Greg had been Colt's best friend and the man had betrayed them all. Seemed like that would make a man leery and unwilling to fully trust. But Colt's relationship with

Danielle had done wonders to heal him on numerous levels.

Still, as the two men walked under the stars on this wintry night, they kept silent for a stretch, maybe considering their next words. For Brent's part, he couldn't get the image of the *cria's* birth from his mind—or Adriana's glowing face. She truly was a beautiful, strong and amazing woman. But Rosa's words, naming the *cria* after her mother, had cut him to the heart.

He started off by explaining that to Colt. "I want to bring down Garcia. I want to bring him down for killing Greg and for all the other crimes he committed. We have to get him, Colt. We can't let him kill that poor girl's parents because she wanted her freedom. We have to get him, whatever it takes." Anger and determination infused his words.

"Whatever it takes," Colt said, angling his head. "Are you sure about that?"

"Dead sure."

"Are you willing to sacrifice Adriana to get him?"

His friend's words gave him pause. He stopped and faced Colt. "She doesn't have to be sacrificed. Why would you even ask me that?"

Colt chuckled. "You've got it bad, man. Real bad."

"What are you talking about?" Brent hoped he wasn't that transparent, even with Colt. Mostly because he had already told himself he couldn't have feelings for this woman. Feelings could get them all killed.

"I think you already know. It's the whole reason why you came here alone to begin with. You think I didn't know that? You wanted her to be innocent, not only because she saved you before, but because you haven't been able to stop thinking about her ever since. Am I right or am I right?" Colt chuckled.

Now it was Brent's turn to chuckle. "I'll agree this has taken a much too personal turn for me. But I can't afford to think about her like that. It's not condoned during an investigation like this, which we both know. And even if we had met some other way, I'm a Texas Ranger. She's the sister of a cartel leader."

"Yeah, yeah. What you're really saying— the meaning behind your words—is that you don't think you're commitment material. And you can't bring yourself to trust anyone that much, especially—*especially*—the sister of a drug lord."

Brent stared at the man. Really. Why did he bother talking if the man could read his mind? That Colt had said it all out loud like that, and revealed all Brent's inner turmoil, rankled.

Before Brent could say anything to counter the other Ranger's words, however, Colt blew out a puffy breath of white vapor and jammed his hands into his pockets. "Matters of the heart aside, Vance said it was your call. If you think she needs to be at a safe house, then so be it. We'll wait here at the ranch for Garcia, if he even knows she's here. But we're going to have to move her fast and without anyone being the wiser."

"I think we have bigger problems than that," Brent said.

"Oh, what's that?"

"I don't think she's going to leave the ranch so easily. She feels safe here—and she doesn't have a lot of reasons to trust the authorities. Forcing her to do anything will not get her cooperation. We need to remain on good terms with her. We need her cooperation if we want to protect her and if we want her testimony against Garcia once we finally catch him."

Colt angled his head and studied Brent. He had an idea of what Colt was thinking—that keeping Adriana on friendly terms—not forcing her to a safe house or forcing her to do anything—was about Brent's relationship with her much more than it was about what they needed to do to close the case. Was Colt right about that? Brent briefly lifted his hat and ran a hand through his hair. Adriana's safety was more important than keeping her happy. He released a heavy sigh.

"Like I said," Colt repeated, "it's your call. Sounds like you've been chewing on that for a while."

"Right. And my call is that we need to move her."

With a big Texas grin, Colt clapped a hand on Brent's shoulder. "Well, if anyone can convince her, it'll be you. I'd advise you to get some rest before you try to use that charm of yours, though. You look terrible."

"Thanks for the compliment."

"Anytime, bro, anytime."

Brent rolled to his back on the lumpy mattress and opened one eye. Bright morning light leaked between the denim curtains, reminding him of where he was. He shot out of bed and reached for his weapon, appalled he'd slept at all.

Then he remembered.

His friends were here. Nearly half of his Ranger team had arrived last night and taken up some of the slack guarding Adriana. They were here to protect her in case Rio Garcia showed up with a small army to take her away and eventually kill her after he found out where she'd hidden the drugs and money—something Brent had yet to learn for himself. As much as they didn't want to face off with Garcia, they wanted him to show so they could arrest him. Though they couldn't be sure that Gregario had delivered the message that he'd found Adriana to Garcia, the chances were high and they would prepare for it.

Major Vance had them walking along a double-edged sword that could kill all of them at any moment.

Brent showered, relieved he hadn't slept most of the morning away, though after the late-night confab the previous evening, as well as watching Kiana give birth, Brent shouldn't blame himself for grabbing much-needed rest.

But now he had a job to do. One he didn't relish.

Since Gregario had shown up yesterday and tried to take Adriana right under Brent's nose, he'd finally made the decision that she should be taken to a safe house. Garcia didn't have to know she'd been moved, and he could still show up here at the llama ranch. They could still catch him with their trap, but Adriana, Inez and Rosa didn't have to be caught in the middle.

Staring into the mirror on the small dresser in the musty room, he swiped a hand down his face. Positioned his earpiece so he could communicate with his Ranger brothers. Convincing Adriana to move to somewhere safe felt like it would be the hardest part of this whole operation. She'd been so adamant before when she said she wouldn't leave. Maybe she saw the need for that now, but he would prepare for a battle, nonetheless.

He clomped down the stairs, the aroma of bacon and eggs wafting up to him and raucous voices that could only belong to his Texas Ranger buddies drifting up, as well. He found Colt and Austin eating at the table, Adriana and Inez serving them like they ran a diner.

Colt stopped midchew, then swallowed. "I told them it wasn't necessary."

Adriana motioned for Brent to sit. He frowned.

"I told your friends that you can't do your job on an empty stomach. Go ahead and eat. Inez and I owe you for protecting us. Eat, then you can go stand guard or whatever it is you do."

Colt pushed from the table. "I'm finished. Come on, Austin. You're finished, too."

Austin scrunched up his face, surprise in his eyes. He still had a full plate to finish. "What? No, I'm not! I don't eat as fast as you."

"Right. That's your second plate."

Austin shoved a little more food in, then his

chair scraped the floor as he stood up quickly, chugged the rest of his coffee and snatched one last piece of toast to chew on. He thanked Adriana, Inez and Rosa as he left with Colt. They'd busied themselves cooking break-fast even after the long night they'd all had. Chances were none of them had slept well, given the very real threat of Garcia's immi-nent arrival at the llama ranch.

Colt bumped into Brent as he passed. "You need to have your talk. We're making arrange-ments."

Brent nodded. *God, please help me to con-vince her this is for the best.*

When Adriana came back into the room with a loaded plate of eggs and chorizo sau-sage on a tortilla with a side of tomato salsa, her eyes held his, and it was as if she could read his mind. Knew he had something to say, something she wouldn't want to hear. Her de-meanor shifted from relaxed to anxious. He didn't miss the slight furrow in her brow, the edge to her lips that only moments before had offered a full-on smile.

He pulled out the chair next to him. "Can you join me?"

"I need to help Rosa and Inez in the kitchen."

"And we need to talk."

"Fine." And, just like that, she pulled out a

chair and sat across from him, instead of taking the chair he'd offered, her face saying she wouldn't agree to anything he would propose. She'd already made up her mind before even hearing his words.

Brilliant work, Brent. And his Ranger brothers were counting on him to get her compliance. Why had he thought she would listen? But he was getting ahead of himself. He wrapped the tortilla around the eggs and spicy chorizo, poured on some salsa and took a big bite. That would keep him chewing while he thought his next words through.

"I'm waiting…" She arched a brow.

He finished up and offered a big grin. She appeared to like his grin, and she visibly relaxed. He was glad he'd taken Colt's advice and gotten some rest before tackling this.

"I know what you're doing. Smiling at me. Turning on the charm. You think I'm so easily swayed." She gave him a smug smile that said, *as if.*

The way she said the words, he could almost think she might be flirting with him. He was glad that Colt wasn't here to see this exchange. His fellow Ranger would start spouting more nonsense about Brent's feelings and how Adriana might return them—as though that mattered, given the circumstances. It wasn't like he could ever take her into his arms and kiss her the way he wanted. It wasn't like they could ever have a life together. Suddenly he lost his appetite and pushed his plate aside to focus.

"Not at all."

"Then say whatever it is you need to say."

"Someone found you here yesterday. You know your life is in danger if you stay. You, Inez and Rosa are all in danger. We can move you to a safe house while we search for your brother. Even give him the chance to show up here. He won't know you've left and he'll come looking for you."

To her credit, she drew in a long, ragged breath, as if taking a few seconds to consider his proposition, before she gave her final answer. He counted those seconds as they went. One one thousand. Two one thousand. Three one thousand...

"No."

"It took you all of three seconds."

It had taken her all of three seconds to answer because she'd already known she wouldn't leave. Adriana couldn't help herself.

"I won't be forced to run away. Not by my brother. Not by you. I'm tired of running. Of being afraid." She went off in Spanish, speaking so fast she was sure she'd lost him.

He held out his hands. Tried to get a word in edgewise, but she wasn't going to let him.

"Adriana… Adriana… I'm… We're only trying to protect you. Protect all of you. What about Inez and Rosa? Maybe they *want* our protection. Maybe they would agree that a safe house is a good idea. Have you thought about asking them?"

"If you want to know their opinions so badly, then ask them yourself. And if they agree to go, then take them away to a safe location. But as for me, I'm staying. Finding Rio will take you a lifetime without me to lure him here. You might think you can fool him, but you're wrong. He'll know I'm not here, believe me, he'll know. He won't come if I don't stay, Brent."

Of course she didn't want to face Rio. Had hoped and prayed it wouldn't come to this. Had wanted to stay here safe and hidden. But that wasn't an option. And now that Rio had finally found her, she couldn't waste any more of her life running and hiding and living in fear.

"And I just can't do this anymore. I'm not willing to spend my whole life hiding from him. Take Rosa, take Inez to your safe house. I'm staying." Anger fueled her tirade, but fear boiled up just under the surface. Fear that she couldn't stick by her words and make a stand.

She'd been terrified yesterday when Gregario had come for her.

Hiding away, waiting for him to leave, she'd been frozen with fear thanks to mental images of being abducted and taken to her brother. Images of the same torture she'd seen inflicted on others now used on her. But then she remembered the others—Brent and Inez—and how could she hide when they could be in danger? She had to end this. Sooner rather than later.

"You're willing to put yourself in danger? Because that's what you'll be doing if you stay."

Her eyes blazed. "If he's coming for me, so be it. I can't wait for this to be over. I can't wait to accomplish my mission in life, to bring Rio and his murderous cartel down." She'd forgotten about that objective for a little while as she'd settled in at the llama ranch and found a peace she'd been missing since her grandfather passed away. She didn't want to die, not yet. But she couldn't live with constantly looking over her shoulder—that was no life. "And besides…if I left and we tried to keep my location secret, we might not succeed. I'm not so sure I can fully trust the authorities. Remember, your friend—the border patrol agent who I have been accused of killing—was working both sides."

Pain flashed in his intense green gaze and pinged against her heart. Why would her words hurt him? Why, indeed, if keeping her safe wasn't personal to him? But, no, she had to be wrong about it. They had that connection from long ago, and the attraction, yes, there was that, but to think Ranger McCord could care about her, really care about her—she was deluding herself yet again. She didn't want that from him. Couldn't have that with him if she did. He was a Texas Ranger. She was connected to a ruthless criminal who was putting all of them in danger.

A part of her wished she had never taken that stupid watch and moved the drugs and money. What kind of crazy must she have been to take on an entire cartel, take on what was left of her family, like that?

But she'd done it and she couldn't turn back now, especially since she'd led others on her path to freedom. Rosa wanted to be free, as well. It was what they both deserved. But they had yet to learn if it was the future God had in store for them. She would just have to wait and see. From this ranch, where the showdown could take place, she should have a pretty good view.

Brent didn't challenge her. Just stood there with his broad shoulders, trim physique, rugged face and compassionate eyes, studying her like he didn't know what to say or how to give her what she needed in any way other than silent support.

And in that, he was giving her the space that she needed and she appreciated that. Adriana turned her back to him. She couldn't take the intensity pouring out of his gaze and his very presence any longer.

"I have to see it through, don't you understand?" she asked, her question a mere whisper.

"I do." His whispered reply came much too close for comfort.

EIGHT

Brent briefly lifted his Stetson to scrape his hair back and skimmed the area beyond the fence where Gregario had tried to take Adriana. He hadn't spoken to Adriana since their discussion this morning, and the sun would soon be setting. His silence had been not so much because he'd been frustrated with her, but because watching the ranch and making sure they were fully prepared for the very real possibility Garcia would show up here required his full attention, as did other Ranger matters. Ranger Ethan Hilliard had gone to watch over Adriana, Inez and Rosa while they were tending to all the llamas and checking on Kiana and Maria.

Brent weighed their options. Did he force the women to a safe house in the face of Adriana's stubbornness? Inez and Rosa had both refused to go if it meant leaving Adriana behind. It wasn't like she didn't understand the danger and brutality she would face if her brother got his hands on her. She'd witnessed that with her own eyes. He would have thought her brush with Gregario and nearly being abducted would have been enough to scare some sense into her—she'd been terrified when she'd run to him from the pasture.

All he could think was that the appearance of the additional Rangers had bolstered her confidence that she could stay here to see it through. But their numbers might not be enough, and not all of them had remained.

Trevor had gone back to Mexico to resume his undercover work in the cartel as he searched for leads on Carmen. Brent found himself wishing that the next time he saw Trevor, the man would have found and assisted Carmen in getting out, and she'd be standing next to him, right as rain.

On the other hand, he had a very real concern that one of their own had already been murdered by the Garcia cartel. Brent couldn't abide that. Sure, they'd all known the risks going in, but he had to ask himself if it would be worth it if things had gone south. If they'd lost Carmen, would the information she'd given them on Garcia prove to have been worth it? So far, he'd have to say no.

He felt Adriana's passion and understood

it—they had to end Garcia's reign of terror, and soon.

God, please let Carmen be okay. Please let us find her if she is...

He stood at the entrance to the odorous barn. Okay, he admitted it. He had been too furious to face Adriana again and had needed to rein in his anger before he even attempted to look into her eyes. Those warm brown eyes. And yet a Bible verse stayed with him all day— don't let the sun set on your anger. He needed to set things right.

He understood her perspective, sure, but that didn't mean he had to like it.

Adriana wouldn't be pressured by him or anyone. She'd survived this long without their help, but his gut told him that her period of safe seclusion was coming to an end.

Especially since she refused to run this time.

He pushed open the barn door and the smell hit him full on, something he hadn't grown accustomed to, even after a few days here on the llama ranch.

Adriana was brushing Kiana down. Ethan was watching over Inez and Rosa in a nearby pasture doing the same for other llamas. A couple of other llamas stood in a corner. Either Adriana hadn't noticed Brent yet, or she refused to acknowledge his appearance. Fine with him. But he was letting out what little warmth the barn afforded them, so he shut the door, then leaned against it and watched her gently stroking the creature.

It was a beautiful image. Mesmerizing, really. He found the woman fascinating. Stunning. Compassionate and courageous. He wished she didn't affect him so much. It wasn't like he'd never met someone with those desirable qualities before. It wasn't like he'd never met a woman he could fall for if he let himself. But his head wouldn't allow his heart to go there. Except, with Adriana, his head didn't seem to have much say in the matter. Why did this forbidden woman stir him like this?

At that moment, she glanced up at him. From the look in her eyes, he could swear she read his thoughts. He wasn't someone to blush, but the slightest rush of heat warmed his cheeks. She focused back on Kiana.

"How are mother and child doing?" he asked.

She angled her face so her curls fell over it as she leaned down to brush, but he could still see her smile. "Doing well, thanks."

At least her tone didn't hold any of her earlier vitriol. Brent pushed from the barn door and moved to stand next to Kiana, who'd grown accustomed to seeing Brent. He grabbed a brush and started grooming the llama's other side. Maria nursed while they brushed. Weren't they just one cozy family?

"You spend a lot of time grooming Kiana. How often do you brush them all?"

She flicked a glance at him over Kiana's back. "As often as needed. We have to keep their coats free of mats and debris. I do spend more time with Kiana. She's always been my favorite, and brushing her relaxes me."

He wasn't exactly sure what to say next, but the day had been long and he hadn't liked the way they'd ended their conversation earlier. "I hope you finally understand that you *can* trust us to protect you."

That hadn't been where he'd wanted to start, but the words were out now.

"If you came here to try again and convince me to live locked away at a safe house, you're wasting your time. My time, too."

She dropped the brush in a bucket and glared at him over Kiana's back. The creature shifted like she could sense Adriana's tension rolling over her. Maybe she could.

He shrugged and kept brushing. "Okay, then. I give up. But let me ask you—is it okay with you that both Rosa and Inez refuse to leave because you're staying? They won't leave without you. So, basically, you're putting them in danger by staying." *Low blow, McCord. Low blow.* But he'd use the tools he'd been given.

Fear flickered in her gaze, but she shuttered it away. "Then I guess you Rangers have your work cut out for you, protecting us here on the ranch."

She grabbed the bucket of grain and hand-fed Kiana while her day-old *cria* continued to nurse.

Touché. "I can see in your eyes that you're worried about them," he said, more gently this time.

"Of course I am. They're my family now." While Kiana ate from her hand, Adriana glanced at Brent and held his gaze.

He thought there might be some kind of hidden meaning behind her words—a question, maybe, about Brent's family, considering he'd chosen to spend Christmas at Adriana's ranch with her small, unusual family. Or he could be reading more into her words than was actually there.

Done with the grooming, he put the brush back and moved to sit on a bale of hay. How did he get somewhere with her, convince her to leave for her own safety without making her mad and shutting her down? He had to admit, he was using a completely different tack with her than the Rangers usually used. "It's pretty amazing that Rosa was able to find you."

"God led her here."

"That might be true, but she used what she knew about you to start." He removed his hat and set it next to him on the bale, combed his fingers through his hat hair. "So why not use her example?"

Adriana angled her head. "What do you mean?"

"Rosa said she thought about what you had told her. That you loved llamas, and that if you had the chance to leave, you'd never go too far away from your home. You even told her you might go just across the border. Maybe you said those things before you thought there was a chance you'd ever leave. Maybe you were dreaming, but that dream came true. You shared enough information that she found you. Granted, it took a lot of determination on her part, and she could have been way off. In the end, you could have just as easily been somewhere else. But she listened to you, and that paid off. Maybe we could end this in some other way than a showdown here at the ranch if you can figure out a way to do the same thing. You grew up with Rio and know more about him than anyone else does. Consider places that are important to your brother. If we can get to him before he comes for you, all the better."

She scoffed a laugh.

Come on, Adriana. Work with me here. "Help us to find him before he comes for you. That's the best way to keep your small family on the llama ranch safe." *And you.* Keeping her safe had become the priority for him. He accepted that protecting her drove him in a fierce, more deeply personal way than he had a right to feel.

Surprising him, she put the bucket of grain down, kissed Kiana's muzzle, then strolled over to sit next to him. Her warmth instantly wrapped around him. The scent of honey from her hair rose up, competing with the barn smells. Her proximity made him dizzy. Uncomfortable. He wished for another place to sit, but even if he had one, he knew he wouldn't move away from her. Next to her was where he wanted to be.

"I appreciate what you're trying to do." She inclined her head to gaze at him, her warm brown eyes taking him in. She had a charm about her, no doubt there, and maybe even knew how to use it, because she was sucking him right in and he was letting her do it. Wouldn't fight it even if he could.

Too bad he wasn't nearly as immune as he'd

like to be. "Oh, yeah? How much do you appreciate it?"

"Any place he might have gone before is a place that I know about, and I'm sure he will have changed everything because of me, his traitorous sister. That's just one more reason he wants me—I know too much about him."

"Don't kid yourself. The best criminal minds make mistakes, and your brother is no different."

"Ah, so you think you know my brother now?"

"Not as well as you. Help me, Adriana. Help me find him before it's too late. To capture and arrest him. We have to explore everything, turn over every stone, as the old saying goes."

She slid from sitting on the bale to sitting on the barn floor, leaning back against the hay. "I'll help you, Ranger man. But I'm going to tell you a story first, that way you'll know me, too. You'll know Rio and you'll know his sister."

"I'm listening," he said.

She drew in a long breath. "My grandfather was a good man as well as a wealthy man. But tough times came. I do not know the reasons behind it. I only know that we found ourselves in poverty. I was too young to remember much, but I remember the anger and the arguments. And going hungry. That fierce pain in my stomach when there was no food except beans all the time. No breakfast or lunch, but beans for supper every day. It wouldn't have been so awful had I not already acquired a taste for the finer things. My father tried to remain true to our belief system, but it turned out having integrity and being a hardworking man didn't put enough food on our table, so when pressured to become a drug runner, he accepted. It changed him in ways I can't even put in words. I think my mother died of a broken heart—all this I took in while under ten years old.

"Then my grandfather died, and I was left to be raised by a drug-running father and an older teenage brother. My father was changed by the work he did. He became cold, uncaring. He had a string of affairs with women he discarded without a second thought. Then he was brutally murdered by a rival cartel and that's when Rio stepped into the business—with nothing but anger, bitterness and vengeance in his heart.

"He rose in the ranks until finally he took over and became more brutal than the head of the rival cartel who'd murdered our father. He was driven by cold and violent anger over our father's murder. At first, he tried to hide it from me, to protect me from it, as though I were too blind or stupid to see. I didn't know him anymore and I was scared of him, though to his credit, he tried to protect me.

"But I could no longer turn a blind eye to what was going on around me. I did what I could to help others in the cartel—those in poverty who were too desperate for a job to fully grasp what they were being asked to do. I mentored those who would receive it in order to escape to a better life—one free of the hopeless choices of either living in poverty or working for the cartel. I did this without him knowing, but I knew the day would come when he would find out and be furious. I walked in terror every day that he would do to me what I'd witnessed him doing to others."

Brent listened intently, hanging on every word. *She's our witness. We have to keep her safe.*

"But that's when I began to see that I should take a chance and escape to freedom myself. But I was paralyzed. After everything I'd seen, I couldn't make a move. I was too scared of the consequences. And then I saw you that day and everything changed. I knew I had to help you, save you from certain death. Still, it was over a year before Rio learned of my betrayal. Someone—Diego—had seen me helping you to escape and kept that to himself, thinking to use it against me if I wouldn't cooperate. He wanted a relationship with me.

"When I refused, he became angry with me and told Rio what I'd done. Rio…he believed Diego over me, his own sister. Never mind that I had lied. If he wouldn't believe me or protect me, then I had to flee. It was what spurred me to act on what was already in my heart. Fearing for my life, I ran. I didn't take much with me. My grandfather's watch, knowing what it held inside and that I could use it to hurt Rio.

"But I would only use my own money— money I earned working odd jobs, baking bread and creating handmade crafts to sell at market—not drug money to escape. And *my* money only took me so far. Everyone on the Mexican side of the border knew who I was. No one would help me. Everyone was scared to help the sister of Rio Garcia as she fled. I thought I would die in the arid region near the border as I worked my way toward the small llama ranch I'd learned about. It had been up for sale, and I dreamed of owning it.

"Seems silly now, that I headed in that direction when I ran, but I had nowhere else to go and it was all I knew to do. I finally crossed the river and there was no one there to stop me. Perhaps I could have gone to the American embassy, since my mother was American, but I feared that, even there, Rio had spies and informants. Besides, how would I even get there in the first place? As it happened, Inez found me, unconscious and dehydrated. She saved my life, and I owe her."

Adriana gazed up at him from where she sat on the barn floor, her long neck exposed. Brent slid down to sit next to her. And dared to look at her. Moisture pooled in her eyes— she'd opened up to him, let herself be transparent and vulnerable. Why?

While he couldn't understand her openness, he couldn't deny that her words had touched his heart, stirring more compassion than he'd known he had. Funny that they would both end up here in this llama barn together. After two years of being grateful to her for how she'd risked her life and thinking of how beautiful she was, he suddenly found himself here, in a position to realize a forbidden dream—he wanted to kiss her. He wanted to take their emotional connection to the next level. It was all he could do to keep from threading his fingers through her hair and cupping her face while he kissed her. *God, help me, I want...*

But I can't. What am I thinking?

It took all his willpower to shove the thoughts away and focus back on Adriana's story.

She'd shared about her family, and that reminded him of his own—part of the reason he could never fully trust or let himself be vulnerable enough to love or be loved. He let the stern reminder that he couldn't get too close to her wash over him, wash away the crazy feelings she stirred in him.

But maybe it was already too late.

"I'm glad you found me that day. I've always been indebted to you."

Sitting so close to him, listening to his soft, compassionate voice, Adriana couldn't breathe. Her feelings for him kept growing, and yet she knew that she—the sister of a drug lord— couldn't fall for a Texas Ranger. It would never work. She hadn't considered that opening up to him would strengthen their inexplicable connection. On the contrary, she'd thought if she told him about her life, he would be repulsed by her and that would drive him away. Force a wedge between them. Prove that they were much too different to be romantically compatible.

Adriana caught her breath. For too long, she'd wondered what it would feel like to be in his strong arms, tugged against his broad chest and held close just because he wanted her there. Because he cherished her.

It was a dream—and it could never be anything more than that. She couldn't let herself hope for it, and she really had to pull back from him right now or she feared she would throw herself into his arms, her lips against his. A warm thrill ran through her, but she pushed it away. Brought herself back to her senses enough that she could distance herself from Brent. Break the moment before it was too late and they shared a kiss. She had a sense that one kiss would forever seal her fate to his.

"There's no need," she said, forcing coldness into her tone. "You don't owe me anything. I knew I couldn't let you die. I knew I had to act, and that set me into motion. First to save you. Then to run—and take the watch. The goal in the end was always to bring down my brother." She couldn't quite force herself to cap off the dismissal with the lie: *it had nothing to do with you.*

She started to get up and push away, but he grabbed her wrist, held tight and gestured for her to stay put. Why she complied, she wasn't sure. She should have taken the chance to at least put space between them, but she didn't.

"You've told me your story. Maybe it would make you feel better if I told you mine."

"Okay." Uncertainty edged her tone. Just why did he feel the need for her to know his past, his life? That wouldn't make her trust him more than she already did. But it might make her care about him more. She wasn't sure that was a good idea, especially as she listened to the deep tones of his rich voice.

He told her stories of his childhood, growing up in a suburb near Baltimore, that made her laugh and then cry a little. Oh, she wished he hadn't shared so much of himself. She didn't want to be tied to him this way. What was he doing to the both of them?

"So, you see, I grew up an only child. We were wealthy, like yours in the beginning. But in the end, it was all a facade."

That made her curious. "Well, don't stop now. I want to know what you mean that it was a facade." Could it be their lives weren't so dissimilar?

"My father turned out to be a criminal, too. Just on a different scale and with different methods. No drugs that I'm aware of. He ran a big corporation—was CEO of McCord Industries, which earned him a big paycheck. But that wasn't enough for him. No. He had to have more and was tried and convicted for embezzlement, insider trading and worse—murder."

She gasped at that. Held his gaze. The depth of pain that lingered there was profound, and compassion for him surged. And unfortunately, their connection deepened, at least on Adriana's side of the equation.

Help me, Jesucristo.

"Murder?"

He nodded. "That's right. Murder. He killed a man who tried to blackmail him. The trial, all of it, ripped our family apart. Before then, I looked up to my father. I dreamed of being like him one day. He raised me to be a business-man. Groomed me to take over the business someday, to follow in his footsteps. But after the trial that laid bare all of his crimes—aired all the proverbial dirty laundry that I hadn't known about before—Mom committed sui-cide. And I couldn't stomach even looking at the man I'd admired my entire life. His be-trayal was too devastating for words."

Adriana hoped he had forgiven the man. No matter what his father had done, Brent needed to forgive, for his own sake—to take that bur-den off his heart. And with that thought, she realized she had to work on forgiving her brother.

"I'm so, so sorry," she whispered, feeling for the man beside her. Their lives weren't much different, after all. Except that, as far as she knew, he wasn't running from a family mem-ber who was trying to kill him.

No, Brent McCord had drastically changed his life. Had found a way to move on.

"So, how did you end up a Texas Ranger?"

He chuckled. "It wasn't planned. I wanted to put as much distance as I could between me and my father and the reminders of the life that had been shattered. I dropped out of college for starters and moved to Texas. I'd become fascinated with the criminal investigation aspects of my father's inquiry—yeah, I know, I wanted to put it behind me, but I let it propel me into my current career. I went to work in law enforcement in Texas, worked in the major crimes division of the Dallas PD before applying to the Texas Rangers. I hadn't been with them very long before I ran into you." He grinned.

Oh, why did he have to grin at her like that?

"So, you see, we're not all that different," she said. "I once looked up to my brother— who always protected me before—like you looked up to your father. We've experienced betrayal by a close family member who became a criminal. Only, your father is not trying to find and murder you."

"True. Nor did I steal from my father, but if he hadn't been investigated and I became part of the business like he wanted after college, I can see how things could have gone a much different direction. Maybe, like you, I would have cut some corners legally in attempts to take my father down, like you're trying to take your brother down."

She laughed. "Oh, now you're reaching, totally reaching."

He slowly leaned closer and took her hand in his, sending a current surging up her arm. "No. *Now* I'm reaching."

Her heart bounced around inside. What did he mean? What was he doing? Adriana knew it was time to break both their physical and emotional connection.

She could easily do that by focusing on her brother. "Thank you for sharing your story, Ranger McCord. My legs are getting numb in this cold. I need to walk around. Now, what were we talking about before?"

If she'd hurt him, he shuttered it away. "We were talking about where your brother might go to hide or regroup. Where we can find him to prevent him from getting to you here, since you refuse to go to a safe house." Frustration edged his words, though he still spoke in the same tender tones he'd used to share his story with her, like he…cherished her.

She shook off the unbidden thought and stood. This time he let her get up. Her heart rate slowed, if only a little. There. That was much better. Now she could actually breathe.

She could think straighter when she wasn't so close to him. "If you really think it would help, then I have a few ideas of places my brother might be found. I can't be certain of anything at this point, of course, but there are a couple of places he might use to retreat and regroup."

Brent rose to join her in pacing the barn. "Let's hear it, then. Anything you can tell me will help."

He'd shifted back into true Ranger mode, which relieved her.

"He has a favorite beach house on the Gulf of California. And there's an old mission in Chihuahua."

"Can you tell us exactly where these are located? We have an agreement to work with the Mexican police in our search for him."

She nodded. "Tell me you're not going." Why had she blurted that out?

"Why?" His green-eyed gaze burned through her, searching for truth and an answer she didn't want to give.

Her heart pounded so hard she was sure it gave her true feelings away, feelings she shouldn't have. Feelings she would have to bury. "You know he would recognize you right off. I'm not going to share the exact locations until you assure me you'll stay here." *With me.*

That grin again. "That can be arranged."

She was in so much trouble that had nothing at all to do with Rio hunting her.

NINE

The next day, Brent was anything but happy. Christopher and Ethan had left to go check out Adriana's ideas regarding where Garcia could be. With Trevor already gone undercover again and searching for Carmen, that meant they were down to four at the ranch—Colt, Austin, Ford and Brent.

There was also the chance that their numbers might drop even further. Vance wasn't satisfied with their waiting at the ranch for Garcia to show up. He might send one of their group off to chase a different lead. Maybe the drug lord knew the Rangers guarded the place and that was what held him off. They walked a dangerous, precarious line between wanting to get their hands on Garcia and protecting his sister from him.

But what if he also knew they were spread too thin today?

Someone could be off in the distance across

the river, watching them and reporting in to Garcia. Brent and his fellow Rangers remained outside, watching the perimeter for most of the unusually chilly day. When Adriana brought him a mug of hot coffee, he wrapped his hands around it.

"You shouldn't be out here," he warned. "But I appreciate it."

Her eyes lit up. "You're out here because of me. What else was I supposed to do? Let you freeze?"

He chuckled.

But her playfulness turned to a grimace. "Seriously, it can't be good for you to be out here in the weather all day."

"I won't lie. I feel the cold all the way to my bones. But I'll live. I'm here to protect you, so I'm going to need you to go back in the house and stay there, Adriana. Just until our Ranger numbers are back up. Please. Don't leave the house again. Someone could take you out or harm you from a distance. You do understand that, right?" *Add to that, you're too much of a distraction for me.*

She nodded and started back.

"And, at any moment, feel free to change your mind and let me take you to a safe house."

"I don't want to be caged like a prisoner." Adriana kept going and didn't wait for his response.

He could understand that she hated being locked away even though it would be in a safe house, when it was her brother who needed to be incarcerated. But if she was imprisoned in her own home anyway, why not go to a safe house?

That evening, he switched out with Austin for a warm meal inside with Inez. What a strange little family they all were, gathered during the holidays for extenuating circumstances beyond imagination.

Refusing to be served, he ladled stew into a bowl. "This isn't necessary, you know."

"I know," Inez said. "You keep telling us that, and yet here you are, eating the stew." Her eyes crinkled with her smile, accenting her warmth-infused eyes. "But I wouldn't have it any other way."

"Where is she?" Brent had hoped to see Adriana when he came to the house.

Inez gestured with her eyes to the ceiling above. "In her room, pouting, I think. She doesn't like this prison of her own home."

"I wouldn't insist if there was another way to keep her safe. But now that her location is likely known, she's too at risk from snipers to be walking around outside."

"She understands, even if she doesn't like it. We both see you're here to protect us. I know you'll do right by my Adriana. I think of her as my own, you know? When she first came to me, bruised and broken, and I cared for her, she filled a hole in my life. My husband has been dead for fifteen years. If it weren't for the llamas, I would've had no reason to keep going, and then Adriana needed me."

"Seems like you needed each other."

Inez patted his arm as she chuckled. "You're right. We needed each other then and we need each other now, especially since we've added poor Rosa to the fold. And we need you, Ranger McCord." Inez pinned him with her gaze.

He suddenly felt the weight of his burden to protect these three women, the responsibility that he'd taken upon himself, made even heavier with Inez's words and her serious expression.

He lowered his soup bowl. "You know to call me Brent, right? I spent Christmas Day with you, remember?" He grinned, hoping to add levity. "So I'd say we're on friendlier terms."

She chuckled. "I don't disagree. But I called you Ranger McCord to remind you of that part of the equation. I'll call you Brent now, since you brought up that you're connected to our little family in a more personal way. I trust you to protect Adriana, even if that means you must take her from here. Do you understand me?"

"I tried that already. She won't go to a safe house. Maybe you should be the one to convince her, Inez."

The woman shook her head. "She's determined to end this here at the llama ranch, I think."

Brent stood taller, suddenly understanding better where this conversation was going. "But you don't want that."

Again, she shook her head. "I think her determination, her stubbornness, has clouded her judgment. And she doesn't want to seem weak. I think maybe...maybe she wants to face off with her brother one last time. Face off with him and win. And that scares me, more than I can express. I don't see how that could end well for her." Sadness filled Inez's eyes.

"Why don't you tell her this? Tell her how scared for her that you are. She respects you and listens to you," he said. "You have more influence over her than I do."

"I have no influence over her—she cares for me, but she is a grown woman who makes her own decisions. Tell me, Ranger McCord. Tell me, Brent, that you can keep her safe if she stays here. That you can keep us all safe. I sense the tension rolling off all of you as you come and go. This is no place to be when Rio Garcia shows up."

"Inez." Her words squeezed his chest. "If you can't talk sense into Adriana, then you and Rosa should go to a safe house. Let me at least take you there."

"Like I could leave her…" Tears pooled in the woman's eyes.

"For Rosa's sake, then."

Frustration boiled in his gut. *Oh, God, please help me to do the right thing. To say the right thing.* Brent wanted to reassure this woman, but he wouldn't lie to her. She deserved his honesty rather than false comfort.

Then Adriana suddenly appeared from around the corner, unshed tears in her eyes. She rushed to Inez and hugged her. When she released the older woman, Adriana looked at them both. "I'm sorry, I eavesdropped. I… I heard you talking about me and I couldn't help it. I waited to hear what you would say. I'm sorry that I've been so selfish, Inez. You're right when you say I want to end this standoff with my brother here at the ranch, but this has been your home for decades. I'm putting your home, you and Rosa in danger by staying. Forgive me."

"There's nothing to forgive," Inez said and hugged Adriana to her again.

of all days, when she might let her guard down a little—than he could if the Texas Rangers descended on the ranch to arrest her for Gunn's murder and the drugs and money she'd taken. And that was exactly what would happen if he made that call. But if he didn't make that call in time—with the proof he needed, the evidence of her innocence—then Garcia's men could descend on the ranch and kill her.

God, please help me find the truth before it's too late.

knew his sister was staying near the border, which had prompted the Rangers to be on the lookout for him.

Brent glanced back at the ranch house, the barn and the distant pasture where thirty or so llamas grazed. The temperature had already reached the high forties and might even reach the fifties. Christmas in Texas was nothing like the white Christmases he used to have in Baltimore where he grew up. But he shoved his past aside and concentrated on the present.

Okay. So, he'd found Adriana. Though it surprised him, that had been his hope and prayer. But Colt would want to know that, too. The Rangers needed to know. Only problem was that they all thought she was guilty of murdering border patrol agent Greg Gunn. Brent needed more information—like if she had an alibi. Something, some kind of evidence, that he could use to prove she was innocent before he called them. And he shouldn't wait too long. That could get them killed. Not just Brent and Adriana, but also the sweet, elderly Inez.

Brent needed his team here, one way or another, but not yet.

And…it was Christmas Day.

Brent just might learn more from her by spending time with her today—this special day

When Inez let go of her, Adriana glanced at Brent. "Take us to this safe house of yours, Ranger McCord."

He grinned, glad they had finally come to an agreement. "I'm glad to hear that." She had no idea how glad. "I'll make all the arrangements. You ladies go ahead and pack a few clothes and personal items. The sooner we get out of here, the better. Please inform Rosa for me, too."

His cell rang, startling them. He glanced at the display. It was Vance. "I have to take this call." Perfect timing. He could arrange for transportation to the safe house.

Adriana and Inez nodded. Inez disappeared into the kitchen to put away the stew bowls, and Adriana headed upstairs presumably to pack. Things were beginning to go their way. Next he would try to persuade her to give up the location of the drugs and the cash. But he doubted that would happen until they nailed Garcia, or until she truly felt safe. Adriana believed the drugs and cash were her only leverage against her brother, should he get his hands on her. Who could blame her?

Brent answered the call. "McCord here."

"Her suggestions paid off…to a point," Vance said.

"What happened?"

"We got our hands on two henchmen at the

old mission—we're working with the Mexican authorities to question them. Haven't heard from Ethan about the bay area. They might not even be there yet."

"The guys snagged at the mission. What did they say? Any hints about where we can find Garcia?"

"No. They won't give him up. Maybe we'll catch up with him at the bay."

Brent opened his mouth to say that Adriana had agreed to move to a safe house...but then he sensed it, felt the whir in his gut an instant before a concussive blast rocked the house. The force throwing his body against the wall.

Whomp.

Wind rushed through her, sucking the oxygen from her lungs. The floor beneath her lifted. The ceiling crumpled. Adriana struggled to stand. To breathe.

The window! She needed to get to the window. To get out of the house that seemed to be collapsing around her!

The tall chest of drawers against the wall toppled toward her. Screams erupted from her throat, but she couldn't hear them over the explosive sound. Nor could she escape the dresser.

Images of Inez, Rosa…and Brent…worry and fear for them accosted her at the same instant she feared her own death. Was it moments away? Time seemed to slow as everything— the walls and the ceiling and the furniture— came crashing down around her.

She dropped to the cracked floor next to the bed and covered her head, uncertain if the floor would fall out from under her. Or if she would be crushed under it all as the world around her exploded and collapsed.

"God, please help us!" But she couldn't hear her own cries, her own screams, for the ringing in her ears.

The dresser crashed into the bed, and when Adriana lifted her head, she realized it had cocooned her. Chunks of the ceiling littered the floor, which blessedly hadn't buckled under her. She stayed still, afraid that movement on her part would cause something to shift. But worry for the others overcame her fear.

"Inez! Rosa!" she called. "Brent!"

Oh, it was no use. With her ears ringing, she couldn't hear anything. Couldn't hear if someone had replied to her call or needed her help. She would have to move from the relative safety of her spot, despite the possible consequences. Carefully, Adriana crawled backward, out from under the cover of the dresser. A hand gripped her arm and pulled her up to stand.

Brent. Momentary relief whooshed through her.

A gash in his temple gushed blood. Dust and plaster coated his face and clothes, turned his hair gray.

"You're hurt." She lifted her hand to touch the wound, then drew back.

He pressed his forefinger to his lips, then pointed out the window. Motioned with his fingers that others were coming.

Others as in the Texas Rangers on the property? Or others as in whoever had planted this bomb right under their noses? But she saw the truth in his worried eyes, in his protective demeanor, as he took her hand, his gun drawn, and pulled her from the room. The staircase had been destroyed.

"Inez, Rosa…" she whispered. Brent watched her lips. "Are they okay?"

"I'll find them." He spoke so she could read his lips, too.

Brent used the structural two-by-fours that were now visible to climb down and then drop to the first floor. He assisted Adriana down as far as he could, then caught her in his arms when she dropped. He set her on her feet.

Though brief, his embrace had been warm and strong.

Reassuring.

He started moving away, but she grabbed him. He turned back to her.

"Where are we going?" she asked.

He looked thoughtful for a moment, then appeared to shake off confusion. "Your hiding place. Where is it?"

Adriana glanced around the destroyed house, grief rendering her paralyzed, fear squeezing her throat. Brent gripped her shoulders and shook her. "Where?"

She pointed down the hallway now blocked with rubble—the remnants of the house. How would they get through the mess? How would they know if the tunnel was still intact? She didn't follow Brent but instead let her gaze search the wreckage. Covered in gray dust, a bloody arm extended out from underneath fallen Sheetrock.

Her heart plummeted.

"Oh, no!" She scrambled over the debris and made her way to the bloodied hand. Removed chunks of furniture and ceiling while hot tears streamed down her face.

Brent appeared at her side and in one fell swoop he moved the pile of Sheetrock and broken two-by-fours.

"Oh, Inez…" For a moment, Adriana couldn't bear to look at her injured friend and turned her face away. *Oh,* Jesucristo, *help her...*

She forced her gaze back to Inez. The woman, her dear friend, deserved Adriana's full attention and aid. This woman had nursed her back to health once, had saved her in more ways than she could put to words. Adriana had brought this suffering down on her. How would she ever get over the guilt?

Brent pressed his hand against Inez's carotid artery. "She's alive."

Adriana actually heard his words this time, but her hearing remained slightly impaired. Gunfire resounded somewhere outside the destroyed home. Palming his weapon, Brent aimed it in the direction from which the shots were coming—the blast had taken out the entire house on that side.

"What are we going to do?" Adriana whispered as she brushed Inez's hair from her forehead. "We can't leave Inez here."

"I'm afraid to move her. We could make her injuries worse."

"And what about Rosa?" Adriana's heart felt like it had been crushed along with everything else in the house. "Rosa!"

"Quiet, Adriana," Brent whispered. "We

don't want to draw the attackers to us. That won't help Inez or Rosa, either."

"Right. Like they aren't already headed this way to make sure I'm dead!" How could this have happened? But she understood their strategy now. Planting a bomb in the house had wreaked havoc. Broken through the protective walls—and made her realize even with the Rangers here, she had never been safe. Had Gregario already planted the bomb when she found him, planning to detonate it with one word from Rio?

Brent's gaze shot around the rubble. "There. I want you to hide in that corner. It looks relatively stable. Get down in there and hide. Let me take care of this."

Adriana nodded, though she wanted to argue. She understood that distracting him wouldn't do either of them any good. She scrambled over to the corner and hid behind the fallen boards. Gunfire rang through the house. Her brother's men were getting closer now. Adriana squeezed her eyes shut and tried to keep from screaming. She was helpless.

Helpless to save her friends.

Helpless to assist Brent.

But she could pray, and she whispered under her breath. "Lord, *Jesucristo*, please save us from the evil in this world. Save us from the men who did this. Please keep Rosa safe, wherever she is, and help Inez to get better. Send help!"

She opened her eyes and peeked through the boards. Another round of gunfire resounded. Brent jerked back with a pained grunt. Had he been hit?

TEN

Pain shot across his upper arm, but Brent ignored it—what choice did he have?—and pushed forward, firing his semiautomatic weapon repeatedly. After a glance back at Adriana to confirm she remained safe in the corner, he exited the house through a window. The porch roof had collapsed, blocking the front door. In the distance, he spotted Colt and Austin closing in on the two men who'd tried to enter the house.

Brent didn't want to leave the women here alone, in case there were others. "Colt, can you hear me?"

When he got no response, he snatched his earpiece out of his ear. The concussive explosion had apparently rendered his radio useless, too. He'd have to trust Colt and Austin could handle the henchmen. In the meantime, Brent made his way around the house, his weapon at the ready, in case more of Garcia's men approached the house from a different direction. Satisfied that no one was approaching for the moment, he found his way back into the house through a back wall that opened into the kitchen. His arm throbbed. He'd have to see to it soon.

In the far corner, he found Rosa huddled, her face pressed into her knees.

She's alive! Thank You, Lord. Brent crunched over the debris and made his way to her. He removed a board that had protected her. "Rosa, it's me, Ranger McCord... Brent."

Shivering, Rosa barely lifted her face. Tears streaked through the grime on her cheeks.

"It's okay." Brent offered his hand. "I'll take you to Adriana."

At those words, hope registered in her gaze, and she stood carefully on shaky legs. He slipped his hand around her waist in case she crumpled to the floor. "Adriana," he called quietly. "I found Rosa. It's all right. You can come out now."

He hoped his words were true. And since he had no way to call, the explosion having taken out his cell and the house phone, he hoped Colt had called emergency services, which unfortunately would take much too long to arrive at this remote ranch. The sound of movement let him know that Adriana had heard him, and she appeared at what used to be the door between the kitchen and dining room. Her face was as dusty and tear-streaked as Rosa's as she rushed forward to grab Rosa into a hug.

The two cried together. Tears of grief, at first, then tears of joy that they had both survived, though he knew Adriana remained devastated over Inez's injury. Keeping aware of his surroundings in case another of Garcia's men showed up, he turned his attention to Inez, making his way back to her.

When he dropped to his knee, he found her lids fluttering.

"Inez, it's me, Brent." He reached for her hand and took it in his. "Can you hear me?"

She squeezed. Good, she could understand him, but for some reason that was all the response she seemed to be able to muster.

"Just hang in there. Help is on the way. Adriana and Rosa are fine. You're going to be fine, too, so just hang on."

Adriana rushed to his side and fell to her knees. She pressed her forehead to Inez's and prayed for her. Her desperate prayer squeezed his heart until he thought he couldn't breathe.

These women had depended on Brent to keep them safe. Had depended on the Texas Rangers and their special task force to guard them from harm at the hands of Rio Garcia and his henchmen. And he had let them down. How had this happened? What had he and the other Rangers missed? When had someone planted the bomb? Guilt and shame at his utter failure tried to consume him.

"Brent." Colt's voice yanked him from his morbid thoughts.

He stood, spotting Colt in the doorway. Colt's gaze fell to Inez and his expression turned even grimmer. "I called for backup and emergency services. I had a feeling we would need a medical helicopter here ASAP."

"They're on their way?" Brent asked.

"Yep. But it'll still take them time. Looks like you didn't come away unscathed." Brent gestured at Brent's head and his arm.

He managed a slight nod.

"Take off your jacket. Let's stop the bleeding."

Good idea. Brent had been so pumped up on adrenaline and trying to protect Adriana, he hadn't taken the time to examine his injury, much less bandage it up. And now a strange numbness fell over him. The adrenaline crash or maybe his body's response to the trauma. Shock.

Colt ripped part of Brent's shirt and made a tourniquet for his arm near his shoulder. Brent steeled himself against the pain. It throbbed and burned, but much worse had happened around him. He hoped the chopper wouldn't take too much time. Inez had abrasions and trauma on the outside, and likely internal injuries, as well. Once again, the guilt strangled him.

Colt grabbed his shoulder. "You can't blame yourself."

"Can't I?" It was easy to do. He couldn't find a loophole that said he wasn't to blame.

"Blaming yourself is only going to cause more problems. We have a job to do and you need to focus. I hear the helicopter now." Colt moved to leave Brent's side.

Brent reached out and snagged him by the wrist. "Those men. Did you catch them?"

"Caught one of them with a bullet. He's dead. The other one got away." Colt swiped his sleeve over his brow. "Austin is standing guard out there."

"They'll be back."

Colt nodded his agreement. "But when they return, we won't be here."

"Why would he try to kill his sister?" Brent lowered his voice. "I thought he needed information from her."

"I don't think killing her was the plan. The dead guy? He had a tranquilizer gun on him. We've had her staying inside for protection. I think they wanted to stir things up and get her out of the house so they could dart her and take her to him. But that plan failed."

"Obviously. They should have been more careful. She could have been killed in that explosion." Brent scowled. "And they really thought they could just tranquilize her and cart her off right under our noses?"

Colt shrugged. "They planted a bomb right under our noses."

"Maybe. Could have been planted before you got here, but had to have been after Gregario discovered her." Brent winced at the pain in his arm—and the pain in his heart at the indication that the bomb had been planted on his watch.

"Don't blame yourself, bro."

Adriana crossed over to them, her expression grim. "What about the llamas? Who's going to care for them now?"

"Don't worry, ma'am," Colt said. "We'll make sure they're well cared for."

"I need to check on Kiana. This explosion could have damaged the barn. She and baby Maria could be injured."

"Ford is checking on them," Colt said. "He's good with animals and I think they can sense that." Colt glanced at Brent, effectively turning this conversation over to him, then made his way to meet the emergency vehicles and chopper.

Brent appreciated his attention to detail. Adriana trembled. In shock, just like Rosa. He didn't think he could find blankets in the rubble, and it would be best to escort the ladies out of the house, but he knew they wouldn't leave Inez alone.

Neither would he.

Gently, he gripped Adriana's shoulders. "The llamas are going to be fine. They aren't the target here. I promise, we'll find someone to care for them. But let's get Inez taken care of first. The medical chopper is here to take her to the hospital."

She nodded. To see this strong woman reduced to trembling silence tore at his insides. Made him furious, not just at himself, but at her brother. The man could have killed his own sister. Maybe her death hadn't been what Rio Garcia wanted, but it had been dangerous and risky to bomb the house. Garcia's men had made a tactical error. He'd guess the one who survived would pay a high price, considering Adriana would now go into hiding after Garcia had only just discovered her location.

And now Garcia would never find her. She would finally be safe.

Brent led Adriana and Rosa out of the house

as Colt and Austin directed the emergency personnel inside to carefully place Inez on a gurney. Another EMT doctored Brent's bleeding temple and his arm, and examined Rosa and Adriana. They were deemed physically unharmed, aside from tinnitus and some bumps and bruises, though the EMT placed blankets around each of the women. It was the psychological damage that had Brent worried, especially when he stood with Adriana and watched her reaction as the EMTs rushed Inez to the life-flight helicopter.

The chopper's rotors started up and wiped away all other sounds. They stood still, watching it fly away into the distance. A county fire truck and the local sheriff's vehicle were now parked next to the Ranger vehicles, and men roamed the destroyed home, looking for fragments of the bomb left behind. Evidence. Brent would leave them to it.

Then Adriana turned to him, grief surging in her eyes. "You and I both know this is my fault." Her voice barely croaked out the words.

"No, that burden falls on me. On the Rangers. We assured you we would protect all of you."

"You tried to convince me to leave, to go to a safe house, and I refused. You and your

friends could only do so much, Ranger Mc-
Cord. I tied your hands. It's my fault."

Why was she referring to him imperson-
ally now?

"You're right. I can only do so much. But
you shouldn't blame yourself." He understood
personally, however, that it was easier said than
done. "Come here."

He drew her into his arms and held her, long
and hard, and somewhere deep inside, a part
of him never wanted to let go. But the logical,
thinking part of him knew he would have to.
He wasn't relationship material. They could
never be together. He would have to let her go
from his mind and his heart.

Eventually. But, in the meantime, he would
savor this moment that she was in his arms,
safe and sound, though traumatized.

And he would devise a plan to take Garcia
down before he killed them all.

Adriana held Inez's limp hand and prayed as
the woman lay in the hospital bed, her smallish, elderly form appearing feeble and pale
with the many tubes coming out of her and
countless wires connected to beeping ma-
chines.

Adriana had been escorted to the hospital by
two Rangers who were not Brent. Of course,

he had responsibilities and couldn't hold Adriana's hand 24/7. She didn't need him to. Didn't want him to. Well, that wasn't entirely true, either. She missed his reassuring presence. Other than Inez, he was the only one she'd let herself trust.

Had trusting him been a mistake?

She didn't want to think he'd let her down, and it certainly hadn't been intentional. He'd done everything humanly possible to protect them. But she felt disappointed anyway. Disappointed in the law enforcement entities' ability to keep her safe—even though she'd known better. She'd known that no one could protect her from Rio. Stupid, stupid girl.

But her trust in Brent went beyond her belief that he could protect her.

Whether she liked it or not, they shared a pivotal moment in their past, and since he had come to the ranch, they had opened up about their lives, as well. She'd never wanted to count on anyone or lean on anyone, setting herself up for heartache. Though they had much more in common than one might think on the surface, she and Brent were still much too different. But how did she let go of a guy she'd had a crush on for two years, especially when he'd ridden into her life like some knight in shining armor wearing a Stetson?

Still, he wasn't here now, and maybe that was for the best.

One of the men on Brent's Ranger team—Ford—had been stationed outside Inez's hospital room to keep her safe in case Rio thought to use her against Adriana. Just more evidence of the trouble Adriana had brought into Inez's life. Maybe she'd been mistaken to come to the hospital and let on just how much the woman meant to her.

At least Rosa, sweet Rosa, was already at the safe house. But that didn't mean she was completely safe. How could *any* of them be safe as long as Rio was still chasing Adriana?

She released Inez's hand and leaned back in the less-than-comfortable chair. She kept hoping the woman would wake up while Adriana was in her room so she wouldn't be frightened by her surroundings, but Adriana had been here for most of the day and knew she couldn't stay much longer. Eventually someone would shuffle her to the designated safe house—a place she should have gone long ago. Before the explosion that almost cost Inez her life. Could have cost them all their lives.

She squeezed her eyes to keep the tears back, but it was no use, they burst out the corners with a fury and rushed down the sides of her face.

Lord, I give this burden to You and ask for Your forgiveness for my mistake that still might cost Inez her life. My mistake that cost us the home on the llama ranch. I don't deserve Your forgiveness, or hers or Rosa's. I don't deserve any grace, but I know You give it freely. Just help me to accept that, because I cannot forgive myself!

She released a long, ragged breath.

I can hardly believe it's come to this...

Her worst fears were coming true—people she cared about were becoming collateral damage whenever they tried to protect her. She couldn't seem to stop the torturous mantra that replayed in her head continually—*It's all my fault.*

She should have left the llama ranch behind her and kept moving as soon as she'd recovered from crossing the border.

And now her head pounded. She was sure it had nothing at all to do with the blast and everything to do with the guilt and shame pressing in against her heart. She leaned forward and hung her head while rubbing her neck. How could she release the pressure? It was just too much.

Oh, please, Inez, open your eyes and forgive me for my selfishness!

Voices—the low, deep tones of men—echoed

in the hallway, then footfalls let her know someone had entered the room. She recognized
Brent's step. Her heart skipped a beat. Yes, she'd
spent enough time with him even to know the
rhythm of his walk. The fact he'd come back
and was here now flooded her with warmth and
relief. Despite her earlier thoughts that it was
best he was gone, she couldn't deny that she
was happier whenever he was close.

He said nothing at all, just waited in the
room with her in silence. Something else she
knew about him was that he was a praying
man. Was he praying now? Was he devastated
over what had happened to Inez? Did he blame
himself, too?

Adriana couldn't let him do that. She lifted
her head and her gaze found his. The pain in
his eyes nearly did her in. She rose from the
chair and closed the distance. But when she
stood mere inches from him, the words failed
her. Would he take her into his arms as he'd
done before? She could hardly fathom just how
much she wanted him to do that. How much
she wanted to press into him, even uninvited,
just to feel the security and warmth that ema-
nated from him.

But she could see a new coldness in his gaze.
Perhaps the situation had forced him to rein

in his emotions. Adriana knew she should do that, as well.

She stepped back, but he snatched her to him. Whispered in her ear. "It's not your fault. I don't want you to blame yourself even one more minute, you hear me? The bomb could have gone off at any time. We aren't sure when it was put there. This is on the Rangers. And since the device was probably planted before the others arrived, that means this is all on me."

Against his chest, she couldn't hold back more hot tears.

He shook her against him, then, "You hear me?"

"Only *Jesucristo* can help me in this, Ranger McCord."

"It's Brent, remember? You and I go way back. We've been through too much. It's… Just call me Brent." Desperation edged his tone.

She snuggled in tighter, the forbidden emotions, the feelings about him she shouldn't have, stirring into a frenzy. "Brent."

He pressed his hand over her hair and ran it through her tangled curls. Even though she'd taken a few minutes to wash her face and dust the dredges of the explosion from her hair, she knew she must still look a mess, but she didn't care. She didn't think he cared, either.

"Tanya." The way he said her alias warned her, reminded her they were still in a public place and she shouldn't give her real name away. She stiffened against him and backed away.

Then she saw it in his eyes. The coldness again—warring against his feelings for her. He cleared his throat. "The Rangers will take you to the safe house. I know you don't want to leave Inez, but it's for her safety and for yours."

"You're not coming?"

He shook his head. "Something's come up. I'm heading into Mexico with a team to recover one of our own."

"A missing Ranger?" she whispered.

He nodded. It was likely more than he should have revealed. "You know the danger for you there, Brent," she warned. "Please…don't go. Stay with me here."

He hung his head, then his gaze found her eyes again. "I can't. Not this time."

And in his eyes she read him easily enough. *Not ever again.*

ELEVEN

Austin and Ford escorted Adriana down the stark white hospital hallway.

Brent watched them go. He'd always hated the sterile atmosphere and smell of antiseptic that characterized hospitals. He scraped a hand over his face and down his scruffy jaw. Dust from the explosion still lingered in his hair, on his clothes—reminders of how he'd let Adriana down. He'd grown too close to her and that had clouded his judgment.

They should have kept more Rangers on the ranch. Shouldn't have sent men chasing after Garcia into Mexico. He could keep listing excuses for their failure. But he couldn't change the outcome now. All he could do was keep his focus on the Garcia Mission. He had no doubt that Adriana had messed with his equilibrium. But he'd fixed that now. He wouldn't work with her in this anymore. The others could protect her.

Head down, she walked between the Rangers.

Would she look back at him? He shouldn't hold on to hope that she would. What was the matter with him? Adriana twisted around and glanced over her shoulder. The way she looked at him, he would have thought the Rangers were escorting her to prison. But then, he supposed a safe house was a prison, of sorts, to some.

Regret and shame filled him. He was a coward. He should at least escort her that far. Say his goodbyes. Because this *had* to be goodbye. It might not be the last time he saw her, but from now on he would keep his distance. And if they caught Garcia, then Brent's interaction with her would be limited, if he had any at all. So this was his final chance to be near her one more time.

"Austin, hold up," he called as he hurried to catch them at the exit doors.

The two Rangers and Adriana turned to face him.

"You stay with Inez," Brent said. "Ford and I can take her."

"You sure?" Austin asked.

"Of course. Why wouldn't I be?"

"Whatever you say," Austin headed back to Inez's room, shaking his head as he went.

Brent took his place next to Adriana. "I'll

see you to the safe house before I go. You don't have a problem with that, do you?"

A tenuous smile crept into her lips. "Of course not, why would I?" Her question echoed his own response to Austin. The three exited the hospital. They'd made a point to dress in plainclothes rather than anything that would identify them as Rangers. Avoid standing out or drawing anyone's eye. With all the various branches of law enforcement out in full force after the incident, it wasn't likely that Garcia's men would pursue them now, especially in town and in broad daylight. But then again, the man was growing desperate. Getting bolder.

The bomb at the house was proof enough of that. So they wouldn't be taking any chances.

The plan had been for them to use a Chevy Silverado pickup belonging to the Rangers for use in covert operations or safe house transportation—nothing about it to identify it as a Rangers' vehicle. On the way to the safe house, he'd switch vehicles again, in case they were being followed. Adriana climbed into the vehicle to sit between Brent and Ford. He turned on the heat to take the edge off the high-forties chill. Then he drove them out of the parking lot through town and onto a lone two-lane highway, heading in the opposite direction of the safe house. When he hit the accelerator, the truck roared to life with a loud rumble. Yeah. He was just another Texas redneck.

"You're taking the long way around?" Ford asked.

"Yep. Need to make sure we're alone when we get there." Brent was done with taking chances. Staying at the llama ranch had been a risk, once they strongly suspected that Garcia had found Adriana. A stupid, dangerous risk. And a poor little old lady was paying the price.

Lord, please help Inez heal and keep her safe. Keep us all safe.

"Look out, Brent," Ford said. "I think we have a tail."

"I see it." An old gray van had been with them since the hospital parking lot. He hadn't been sure if the van was following them, but now his suspicions inched higher. This was the main reason he'd taken the long way around to the safe house. He wouldn't want to lead anyone in the right direction.

But he also didn't want to let them know they'd been made because that could escalate their timeline. Brent wanted to maintain control of the situation and act when he was good and ready.

"What are we going to do?" Adriana's voice shook with her question. She'd suffered trauma, as had Brent, earlier in the day, so it wasn't unexpected that her nerves were frazzled. Still, he hated hearing the fear in her voice.

"We're going to survive, that's what."

She started to turn around, but Ford gripped her shoulder.

"Don't look," Brent said. "Let them believe we're leading them to the safe house. Ford, call Austin and let him know someone followed us from the hospital. They could very well be preparing to grab Inez in her room to use as leverage. Get ahold of Colt. Tell him what's going on." Their hidden radios with earpieces and mics didn't work at this distance.

"I'll see if we can get some local law on them."

"No." The word came out too emphatically. "Not yet. Local law will only scare them off and they'll come back later or try the direct approach. But we do need to apprehend them, if possible." If they played this right, they could capture the men in the van without endangering Adriana. If not in the small town he approached, then the next one or the next.

"If you can watch them through your mirror," Brent told Ford, "see if you can figure out how many are inside the van. Getting Adriana to safety is our priority, but we want to take down as many of Garcia's men as we can in the process. These guys could give us information. If they were supposed to take her to Garcia, then they might know his current location."

Brent slowed as he entered the small town. Maybe he could trap them. But he didn't want to engage them in a way that risked anyone getting hurt, including innocents in town.

"Then what's your plan?"

"Give me time to think and more information to go on."

Flashing lights and a siren erupted behind the van as it sped too fast through a school zone. Brent banged the steering wheel in frustration. The decision had been taken out of his hands now. He slowed even further to see what the van decided to do. Pulling over wasn't likely an option for them.

The van sped up and gunfire poured out the back. The police cruiser swerved and crashed into an electric pole. The men were determined to take Adriana at all costs, not even letting law enforcement stand in their way. Garcia's demand for them to return with his sister must have emboldened them. Tension corded Brent's neck and shoulders at their audacity.

As he sped forward, the grille of the van grew bigger in the rearview mirror and weapons appeared out the windows.

* * *

"Get down!"

Adriana ducked even as Brent pressed her head forward toward her lap. Automatic gunfire resounded behind them. Punching the accelerator, Brent steered the truck through the small town along Main Street, bumping over potholes and curbs.

The back window cracked into a spiderweb when a bullet passed through and slammed into the dash. Adriana covered her head with her hands and stayed low. She held back the scream building up in her throat.

Ford twisted in the seat and returned fire. "Got any brilliant ideas, McCord?"

Brent yanked the wheel to the right to make a sharp turn. The tires squealed. "Still trying to lose 'em!"

"I don't think it's working." Adriana didn't want to distract him, but it was clear that they needed another plan.

Brent turned down a backstreet between two old brick buildings. The building on the left was an abandoned warehouse. Wind blew trash around in the alley.

"What are you doing, man? You're going to get us trapped."

"Nope. You're going to keep going and drive out the end of the alley. I'll take Adriana with me. You lead them out of here straight to the police station. I'll hide Adriana here with me and keep her safe. You take care, Ford, and get to the local law. I'm sorry I opted not to call them to begin with. Are you good with this?"

"You know I am. It's okay. Just go and do what you have to do. Keep her safe," Ford said.

Brent scrambled out of the truck. He broke out an already cracked window in the old warehouse, the glass shattering forward into the building.

He practically lifted Adriana from the cab of the truck and stuck her through the window. "Careful now. Watch the glass."

He climbed through behind her. Grabbing her hand, he led her down the dusty hallways of the warehouse—decades old and gutted. They had no way of telling what it had once stored.

In the distance they could hear the Chevy roaring as it took off, and it wasn't long before the van rumbled through the alley after the Chevy. So far his plan seemed to be working. But they shouldn't let their guard down just yet.

His weapon out, Brent led her up the stairs to an empty office and watched out the window. Not too far off, they could hear automatic gunfire again. Concern for the Ranger brother they'd just sent off alone gripped her, and she could see that Brent was concerned, too.

She slid to the floor and sucked in a breath. "Was it safe to leave him like that? What if something happens to him?"

"Ford knows what he's doing. Hear those sirens? The van of punks isn't going to get very far. But I couldn't risk you getting hurt in the crossfire." Brent obviously decided to join her and slid to the floor next to her. "I won't let them take you. I'll die first."

She hung her head. A knot formed in her stomach. "That's exactly what I'm afraid of, Brent. People dying because of me." She stiffened. "Can you call the hospital, check on Inez for me? Can you check on Rosa at the safe house, too? Maybe these guys found it already."

Please, Jesucristo, *let that not be the case!*

While he made the calls, Adriana listened. Her nose tickled from the dust and mold in the old building. She could hear the voices echoing over the phone clearly enough to understand the words. Austin guarded Inez's door and was preparing to switch out with another Ranger. No troubles at the hospital so far.

He contacted the Rangers at the safe house to check on Rosa. All remained clear there, but he warned them about expecting trouble.

Brent glanced at her, a gentleness in his gaze. "You heard all that?"

"Yes. Thank you for checking for me." Of course, it was his job to make sure the women remained safe, so she shouldn't take his actions too personally.

Then Brent called Ford. "You okay?"

"Yeah," Ford said. "Officers have taken the van and captured the men. They know we want to question them and will hold them for us. So I'm coming back to pick you up. It was a good plan, McCord. You did good. Now, if we could just figure out how to get her to that safe house."

The Ranger had put words to Adriana's concerns. How were they going to get her to the safe house without being followed? It seemed Rio was doing everything in his power to keep his sights on her and not let her disappear now that he'd finally found her.

When Brent ended the call, his cell rang. She glanced at his phone with him and saw that Colt was on the line. Adriana was glad she sat close enough to Brent that she could hear the conversations in the quiet room.

"Heard from Major Vance. We have yet another lead on Carmen. We need to check all of them out, which means more Rangers gone to check and that will spread us thin."

"So what's the plan?" Brent spoke into his cell and watched Adriana, reassurance in his gaze.

"With the security detail in place at the safe house, once Adriana is there with Rosa, we'll team up to follow the leads. You're with me. Wrap it up there and get Adriana to the house. We can question those men later."

Brent explained they were waiting on Ford to pick them up. He ended the call and huffed out his frustration.

"What about Rio?" she asked. "Have you given up on finding him?"

Because she would never be safe until he was incarcerated.

He grabbed her hand and squeezed. "Of course not, but we can't forget about one of our own who's in trouble. I just need to get you to the safe house. One thing at a time."

"Getting me there is turning out to be harder than we thought. They must have been watching us this whole time. Knew that I was at the hospital with Inez." A shiver ran over her.

He squeezed her to him and rubbed her arm to send the shivers away. Adriana had thought she would never sit so close to him or hold his hand again, considering the way he'd acted at the hospital.

She heard the Chevy's approach. Brent stood

and held his hand out. She took it and got to her feet to join him. He never let on that his recent gunshot wound slowed him in the least. It seemed nothing could stop Ranger Brent Mc-Cord. She admired this man too much for her own good.

As he led her through the door, Adriana suddenly stopped and Brent lingered in the doorway with her.

"Thank you, Brent McCord. Thank you for keeping us safe. If you hadn't been there when that bomb went off, Rio's men would have us all by now, I'm sure of it."

His face twisted. "It never should have happened. We let them get through our defenses."

"I'm safe with you. I trust you, but I understand why you want to go into Mexico. Why you want to go away from me."

He angled his head. "You do?"

"Yes. It's because of this thing between us. You think it's wrong. You can't let yourself love, and even if you could, you can't be with me, the sister of the leader of a drug cartel."

The truth of her words reflected in his gaze. She'd held on to hope that he would dispute her. Would she ever stop wishing and hoping for the impossible? When she started to move from the door, he held her there, his hands resting on her waist.

He glanced up, then back at her with a half smile. "There's no mistletoe here, like at the house."

"No…" What was he getting at?

He drew in a breath.

"Your friend is probably wondering where we are," she reminded him.

"Probably." His cell rang. He glanced at it and laughed. Answered it. "Be there in a minute."

Jammed it back in his pocket. "Now, where were we?"

"I'm not sure." But she thought she had an idea. "But you mentioned the mistletoe. Inez put it there to trick us."

He lifted her hand up to his lips and kissed it. "I shouldn't do this."

Oh, but I want you to… "*We* shouldn't do this."

But she inched her chin up higher, closer. The thought of what it would be like to kiss Ranger Brent McCord had never left her thoughts since they'd first stood under that mistletoe. If she were completely honest with herself, she had long wondered what it would be like to kiss this man. "We wouldn't want to disappoint Inez."

And Brent met her halfway, pressing his lips

to hers, in a tender, gentle kiss that told Adriana all she needed to know.

They were meant for each other but could never be together.

TWELVE

What am I doing?

Brent shoved away the guilt and allowed himself this one moment in time with Adriana—a woman he'd dreamed of kissing for the last two years. He'd only been this close to her in his dreams. He shouldn't be this close to her now.

But he had a feeling this would be his last chance. And he couldn't let it pass him by.

Gunfire echoed outside, and he tore his lips away. Heart pounding, he tugged her behind him and out of the hallway.

"Oh, no, Brent. What about Ford?"

"Shh," he whispered in her ear.

He didn't like this. Brent called Ford and it went to voice mail.

"Call me!" He left a message. Dragging Adriana with him, he moved to the window and carefully looked outside.

Saw nothing.

*God, please help us. Please keep Ford safe
and help us escape. Help me keep Adriana
safe.* Why was this turning out to be the most
difficult mission of his life?

"What are we going to do?"

"We have to get out of here." They should
already have been gone by now. Once again,
he'd let the way Adriana affected him cloud
his judgment. Still, had they gone outside believing they were safe, they could have been
ambushed and killed.

"I think we should stay and hide until it's
over. Until backup gets here. The police must
know about the gunfire," she said.

It was one thing to hide in the building and
let Ford lead those men away from them, and
quite another to be stuck inside and have Garcia's men closing in. And he had no doubt the
men were sent by Garcia, who obviously had
cartel operatives in Texas already.

"They might be occupied with the others,
and it might take too long. If we stay in this
building, we're going to get trapped. Come
on."

He led her out of the room and down the
hall to the stairs. Brent quietly opened the door
and checked the stairwell. Empty. Together
they bounded down the steps. When they
reached the exit on the first floor, he eased it

open. He poked his head out and saw nothing in either direction.

More gunfire resounded outside. Good. That meant Ford and possibly other law enforcement officers were around to engage Garcia's men. That they'd come for Adriana in this small town should terrify her.

It terrified him.

"This way." He led her down the hallway to the back of the building, then hung a right. They could sneak out into the same alley, through the same broken window they'd climbed through. Brent assisted Adriana through the opening. He felt more exposed than ever in this alley, but somehow Garcia's men had figured out Brent and Adriana were hiding in the building. That was probably because Ford had stopped next to it and waited to pick them up. They'd made the wrong assumption, believing that the police had nabbed all the men when they'd taken the van. Someone else had been in the mix. Someone they'd missed.

Would he ever get ahead and *stay* ahead in this?

Angry voices shouted from both ends of the alley. Looking back through the window, he saw someone inside the warehouse they'd just exited. Someone searching for them.

Not good. Not good at all.

They had no choice but to keep going.

At the corner, the edge of the building, he pressed his back against the wall, Adriana next to him. He held his weapon up. Sweat beaded on his back and forehead, despite the chill of this winter day.

Brent slowly peered around the corner.

"I'm scared," she whispered.

He barely heard her whisper and wasn't sure if she'd meant for him to hear. He squeezed her hand. And stepped around the corner. Together they walked hand in hand, like a couple just out enjoying the day, except nobody was on the street now because of the gunfire. People had taken cover. Law enforcement was on the way. They had to be.

He heard the sirens in the distance.

Too Far. Much too far.

A vehicle turned the corner. An old beat-up sedan. It sped up and headed right for them. More of Garcia's gun-wielding men. They should have received intel that this many men were already here in Texas or would be coming across the border into Texas for Adriana.

He shoved her behind a parked car, returning fire as he took cover, too.

"They're tearing up this town to prevent you from taking me to the safe house. He knows he'll never get a better chance to get his hands on me."

Footfalls sounded behind them. Brent turned in time to receive a fist to his face, then a gun to his temple.

The henchman gripped Adriana's arm so hard she cried out as he yelled in Spanish. Brent understood every terrifying word. "Garcia finally has his sister back now."

The man yanked her along with him as he ran to the car. Adriana fought, but it was no use. Her screams cut through Brent like a dull knife. He chased them.

Sirens grew louder. The police were only a block or two away. But that was still too far.

"No!" Brent yelled and finally tackled the man, smashing against him as they both fell hard on the asphalt. Pain shot through his body and burned like fire across his gunshot wound. Brent ignored the pain and pounded the man's face into the road. Then he stood up to run after Adriana.

Someone from the vehicle shot at Brent. A force slammed into his chest, knocking him onto his back as his breath whooshed from him.

Adriana screamed as they threw her into the car and sped away.

Brent couldn't breathe, much less move.

He heard the familiar sound of a truck's loud muffler and exhaust resounding like a hot rod. That gave him hope. The noisy truck sounded louder, closer, than the sirens that sounded like they were growing distant.

A hand gripped his as Ford's face filled his vision. Helped him up. "You okay, buddy?"

"Alive." Only because of his body armor. "They took her."

"Then let's go get her back." Brent appreciated Ford's positive can-do words. They couldn't afford to think any differently now.

Ford started for the driver's side.

"Let me drive." The pressure in his chest ached, but he was going to drive.

"You sure?"

"Positive." He'd let the fury and rage coursing through his veins forge the way. He tore off his damaged vest, and though it hurt like a firestorm had rained down on him, he ignored the pain, shifted into Drive like a maniac and floored it.

"I don't know what the law enforcement in this town was after, going in the other direction, but they'd better be heading after these guys in the Impala now. We cannot lose sight of them or let them take Adriana."

Hurt her.

Brent couldn't recall ever facing a more determined criminal element.

Ford got on his cell and informed the local police they were in pursuit. Apparently, after arresting the shooters in the van, the police had been called away for gunshots heard in another part of town. Brent shared a brief glance with Ford. Had it been a calculated distraction to pull the police away? The way these men had swarmed into this town in pursuit of Adriana, they might very well intend to break their friends out of jail.

The Impala raced down the highway and Brent followed in the truck. He floored it, swerving around slower traffic at breakneck speed and receiving blaring horns for his efforts. The Chevy truck inched closer, gaining on the men speeding along the highway. Before long, Texas State Troopers appeared on the road in pursuit, as well.

Except Brent was closer. The men in the Impala fired their automatic weapons, shattering the Chevy's windshield. Cold air filled the cab, but Brent ignored the pain it triggered in his chest, the chill reaching to his bones, and focused on getting Adriana.

God, help me!

He could see her in the back seat of the vehicle in front of him. The wind had whipped up her crazy curly hair. She turned to glance at him, and the pleading in her expression could undo him.

Focus, man. Focus!

Then she looked at him again and he saw something much different.

Determination.

Adriana had found her strength again. The same strength that had risked death to save him that day. The same strength that had propelled her to flee her brother. Two of the men were focused on firing their weapons at Brent and Ford. They weren't watching their captive.

Adriana hurled herself forward at the driver.

The Impala swerved, fishtailed, then went completely out of control.

It flipped. Over and over and over.

"No!"

She would never let them take her to Rio. She'd rather die.

The world spun around her. Knowing what she'd planned could be fatal, she'd wrapped the seat belt around her arm. Now she wasn't sure that had been the best of ideas, but it kept her body from being tossed from the car. Instead, she slammed from the seat to the roof as it rolled. The impact forced the breath from her lungs as she bounced back and forth. Seat.

Cab. Seat. Cab. Her arm felt as if it were being ripped from her body. Screams erupted around her. Men's screams mingled with her own.

Then all was still. Seconds ticked by before her head stopped spinning.

Quiet had taken the place of gunfire and the foul language spewing from the beasts who'd abducted her.

Adriana was somehow folded down on the floorboard of the front seat, her arm no longer secured by the seat belt. She presumed the man who'd been sitting here had flown out the window. Nausea roiled as she blinked her eyes open. A hawk screeched from the sky like nothing had happened. Like it was just a normal day.

The driver, the man she'd accosted, was pressed into the steering wheel, blood on his face.

She had blood on her.

Was it hers?

Voices spoke in the distance, growing louder. But they were voices of worry and concern. Not voices of hate and anger. Not bloodthirsty voices.

Relief rushed through her. She could float from that relief. Except she was pinned in this position, somehow. She realized she couldn't easily crawl up from the floorboard, given the way the seat and the dash were awkwardly pushed together. In fact, she couldn't move at all.

"Tanya!" Fear and desperation edged Brent's tone.

The sound of it comforted her, washed away the dread. Tears leaked from the corners of her eyes and somehow even that hurt. Just to cry made her ache all over, the pain of the ordeal finally registering in her mind.

"Tanya, are you okay?" A hand reached through the open window.

"Yes," she squeaked out. "Yes!" Louder this time. "But…but I'm stuck in here. Please… please get me out."

Adriana wanted to sob. But she was absolutely tired of crying. Tired of being weak. She'd made it this far, survived this far. Her brother's men had come all the way into Texas to drag her back to Mexico. She'd never come so close to being taken back, to torture and certain death. And now she was glad she'd risked everything to prevent that from happening.

"Hang in there. I'm going to get you out."

Sirens resounded. Other voices. Other law officers. The State Troopers. An ambulance, perhaps for Rio's men—the ones who had survived.

Brent and Ford argued with another man.

"Jaws of Life," a man said. "We'll have to cut her out."

Brent got close to her again and stretched his arm out to touch her. By his pinched expression she could tell the effort hurt him. He grabbed her hand. "I'm here, honey. I'm here. I'm not going anywhere. You're going to be all right. Please, just stay calm. Are you sure you're not hurt?"

"I don't think anything's broken. I'm not bleeding. Bruised maybe. Pinned for certain." She couldn't help herself. She smiled and cried at the same time. "I saw him shoot you. I saw you fall."

"My body armor, honey. It saved me."

If only she could wipe her face, wipe the tears away, but her other hand was stuck, and she absolutely wasn't going to let go of Brent's hand. "I know, I know. But at the time, I thought he'd killed you."

"But he didn't kill me. I'm here, right here with you."

Her teeth chattered. "I'm cold."

"I'll take care of it, honey."

He had never called her honey before, but she liked hearing it. If only for this moment in time. She reminded herself that they could never be together.

"Shock," someone behind Brent said. "Blanket. We need a blanket!"

A few minutes passed and finally a blanket was shoved through the window and over her, but Brent never let go of her hand. He had to be seriously hurting by now.

"Okay, honey, they're going to cut you out now. So you know I don't want to let you go, but I'm going to let go of your hand just for a minute."

For the first time since the wreck, panic set in. Brent had been her lifeline. "No, no, no, no…"

Brent argued with two other men, his words vehement.

"Okay, honey, I've worked it out with them. I'm right here with you. I won't let go unless I have to for maybe a few seconds while they cut around me, okay?"

Adriana nodded. She squeezed her eyes shut and prayed. She'd survived.

Thank You, Jesucristo.

"Inez, tell me about Inez."

"She's fine," Brent assured her. "She's good. We're moving her to another facility. It'll be harder for you to go and see her, but she'll be more protected. After what went down today, we can't take the risk of her being targeted. Preparations to move her are already under way."

A warm feeling settled in her stomach. "Thank you," she whispered, uncertain if he could hear her. "And Rosa?"

"Still safe. You're going to be safe, too, in a few minutes."

And Brent's words came true.

Though it had taken longer than expected to cut away the door and the roof of the car, and remove the seat, Adriana was finally free of the vehicle. She was immediately placed on a gurney and taken in an ambulance to a small hospital, where she would be examined. Brent rode with her in the ambulance. He smiled down at her, still holding her hand.

Seemed like he was more attentive than any Texas Ranger should be. The others had likely noticed by now, if they hadn't before.

"You're going to be just fine," he told her, squeezing her hand. "This is just a precaution, you hear me?"

Was he trying to convince himself? The worry in his eyes, despite his smile, scared her a little.

"Go ahead and tell her she's okay," Brent said to the EMT.

"We won't know anything for sure until the doctor examines you. You might have some internal bruising, but your blood pressure and heart rate and everything else look good."

"My arm doesn't feel so good."

"I can't tell for sure without an X-ray, but it doesn't appear to be broken. May just be sore for a few days like the rest of your body. You're fortunate to have survived."

She nodded, the news giving her comfort. "And what about the others? The men who abducted me?"

Brent released a heavy sigh. "Out of the four men, only one survived—the one who was thrown from the car. You took a big risk. A dangerous risk."

"I couldn't let them take me to Rio. I would rather die."

Brent's features pinched. Neither of them had expected to take on a whole army in a small town in the middle of the day.

"I'm sorry you felt that was your only option. I take full responsibility for that."

"Brent… I don't blame you."

"That's good to know." But his eyes said something different—*Maybe you should.*

I blame myself. I blame my brother. But never you.

"Once the doctor examines you and gives the go-ahead, we're going to be heading out to the safe house quickly. We're passing up the nearest hospital to keep you out of the line of fire—" he glanced at the EMT "—so that's why it's taking some time to get there."

"I'm beginning to wonder if that's possible."

"What?"

"Keeping me out of the line of fire. I never thought Rio would expend so much energy on me."

"Well, you still possess something he wants." His look was pensive. "Don't you?"

"How come you haven't tried harder to find out where I hid everything I took from that warehouse?"

"I've been waiting for you to tell me—when you were ready."

His words touched her. She could hardly believe them. But that had to be the truth. She flicked her gaze at the EMT, who acted as if he wasn't listening. Right. She couldn't tell Brent now. Even though he hadn't pressured her, she wasn't ready to tell him anyway. Not yet.

Brent squeezed her hand hard. She searched his eyes and saw that he had a lot more he wanted to say that had nothing at all to do with the hidden drugs and money, but something was holding him back. Maybe he could never say the words. But she thought he might have been as devastated when he'd seen the car flip as she'd been when she watched him fall from a gunshot. A tear slipped down her cheek.

He wiped it away. The simple gesture had her heart rate spiking and the EMT frowning.

Oh, don't do that. Please don't do that. I can't be in love with you. We can't love each other.

THIRTEEN

"We have to go." Colt leaned close and lowered his voice.

He clutched Brent's arm and squeezed annoyingly as he tried to drag Brent out the door of the safe house where they had finally deposited Adriana. But Brent resisted even though they were behind schedule to go chase down the lead on Carmen.

Their intel would be of no use if they didn't act on it, and now.

Brent was still attempting to grasp the fact that they'd finally made it to the safe house. Garcia's men had been determined to keep that from happening. Likely they had been tasked with snagging her from the ranch, and failing that, they had resorted to blatant violence in broad daylight.

Colt was trying to drag him out the door before he'd given Adriana a proper goodbye.

A proper goodbye?

What was he thinking?

She was still hugging Rosa, obviously glad to be reunited with her young mentee and oblivious to the fact that Brent was being forced to make a fast exit. He struggled to let her go. Struggled to trust her to the security detail at the safe house, especially after what they'd been through. But maybe she was better off with other, worthier protectors. He'd let her down so many times. He would always be thankful, always be grateful that she had survived, in spite of his shortcomings.

Thank You, God! Thank You... His heart was bursting with gratitude.

He'd thought his heart would fail when he saw the Impala flip repeatedly. Only two of the passengers had survived—Adriana, with her gutsy, risky move and one of her abductors. He was in critical condition and had not regained consciousness, so they hadn't been able to interrogate him.

Adriana hadn't come away unscathed. She'd received a few bruises for her efforts, but that was nothing compared to the injuries she could have sustained, including mortal wounds. Given the extenuating circumstances and because Adriana's injuries weren't serious, she had been quickly released back into the Texas Rangers' hands so they could attempt her secure escort to safety once again.

And this time they had used a chopper to whisk her away and out of Garcia's reach. For the moment.

He squeezed his eyes shut. His heart beat more steadily now, but it wasn't over. Not by a long shot. She wouldn't be safe as long as Garcia was at large. But protecting her from her brother was no longer his responsibility.

Colt finally dragged him completely out the door and Brent yanked his arm free. "All right, already."

He marched with Colt to the SUV they were taking deep into Mexico.

"She's going to be all right. We've beefed up security around the house." Colt tried to reassure Brent. "It's in the middle of nowhere, so nobody can find her out here."

Colt's words, meant to reassure Brent, missed their mark. After the debacle in the small town, Brent had been shaken to his core. Protecting the border and fighting the cartel was ugly business, as ugly as it got, but Brent had never been so personally invested.

"I don't know if our efforts are going to be enough to keep her safe. That was a small army back there. We're playing with a fire like nothing we've ever seen before—a cartel leader bent on getting his sister back. Bent on getting his drugs and money back."

"I've seen a lot in my experience." Colt shifted into Reverse and backed out. "But you're right. Not sure anything can top this. But you've gotten too deep into this to think clearly. I don't think—"

"I can handle it." Brent cut him off.

"I'm not sure Vance would agree." Colt steered the vehicle onto the highway that would take them to the border.

"What have you told him?" Brent angled his head toward his closest friend, hoping the man hadn't betrayed him. There'd been way too much of that going on lately for comfort. A reminder to Brent that he could never truly trust anyone.

"Nothing. But others have seen how you act around her. And once Vance sees for himself, you won't be able to hide that you have strong feelings for this woman."

"Well, it's not like it's the first time one of us has fallen for a woman closely tied to our investigative efforts." Brent turned his face straight ahead, but his eyes flicked to Colt in the driver's seat. Who was Colt to talk to him about being in too deep? Who were any of them?

"Doesn't make it right. Makes us weaker, if you ask me."

"I don't need to say it—"

"But you didn't ask me. I know," Colt said.

"No, I didn't, but I agree with you one hundred percent. My emotions are clouding my judgment. I'll admit it freely, but I can't seem to rein them in. If I'm anywhere near her, a fog moves into my brain."

"A pleasant fog, I'm guessing."

"You know it. But I have to kill it while I can. Before it's too late. That said, I don't trust anyone to be as invested in protecting that woman as I am." *I'd die for her. And I pray it doesn't come to that, because even though I know I can't spend the rest of my life with her, I can't think of anything else I'd rather do.* "Let's get Garcia and be done with it so there's no reason I need to see her again. I won't even go back to the safe house after we're done following up on these leads. I'll let you guys handle that part of it." Brent cleared his throat, cleared away the emotion that grew thick at his harsh words. They pained him. Nothing about them sounded right.

"Whatever you say." Colt didn't sound convinced.

Brent changed the subject. "How's Danielle?"

"She's doing well. I'd like to get back and see her as soon as I can. I think we've started a good thing, and I'd hate to have a mission take me away from her for too long. And this Garcia Mission can't be over soon enough, again, if you ask me." He chuckled.

Brent allowed himself to relax and laugh a little, too. They had a long night ahead of them. So much had happened in the last few days, he felt like it had been a year and not a week. "Let's hope we have it all wrapped up before New Year's so we can be on to something different by next year."

"That's just two days away."

"Yeah. I won't lie and say I'm confident we'll have Garcia in custody by then." Initially their mission had been to prevent him from crossing the border, but with the crimes he'd committed against American citizens, including murder, they wanted to arrest him. Try him in the United States. "We just need to get ahead of this guy, Colt. Right now I feel like we're two steps behind him."

"Why don't you get some rest, buddy. We have a long drive before we hit the border. And we've got our work cut out for us."

God, please let us find Carmen alive and bring her home this time. Brent settled into the seat, putting it in a reclining position, and covered his face with his hat.

Though exhausted beyond words, he couldn't

easily fall asleep, his mind going right to that forbidden kiss he'd shared with Adriana, the woman he'd dreamed about since he first laid eyes on her two years ago. He'd let his heart go free a little in that kiss. To be honest, it had already been halfway out of the cage, eager to be set completely free to love when he'd found her alive in that vehicle. Somehow he had to distance himself from her. He didn't have it in him to trust anyone enough to truly love them, and she deserved much more than he could ever give her.

Brent woke up as they approached the border. Working with the Mexican authorities via their task force, they were able to enter Mexico to work covertly and bring their weapons with them.

Brent's cell rang. "Vance, what's up?" He put the call on speakerphone.

"Heard from Trevor. We got some new intel. All our leads are dead, including the one you were going to check out. But we have a new one and let's hope this is it. Let's hope this will be the one to bring Carmen home." Desperation edged Vance's tone.

They all had this feeling that with each dead end, the chances of bringing Carmen home alive dwindled further. The news dropped into Brent's gut like too many bags of concrete.

"Well, what is it?" Colt asked.

"You're not going to like it. Our informant said he heard of a woman who jumped off a cliff into the Gulf of Mexico. Someone found her still alive. She's in a village near the Gulf."

Vance named the village, and Brent scraped a hand down his face. "That'll take us all night to get there."

"Are you complaining, Ranger?"

"No. Just stating the facts. I hope this is it. I hope we find her."

"You know we'll do our best," Colt added. "We're on it. Give us the coordinates."

Vance replied with the information, which Brent plugged into the GPS.

"Sounds like she was heading for Brownsville, trying to get back across the border. They must have been chasing her down hard. What's the rest of the story, Vance? Just how bad was it for her to have jumped off a cliff?" He probably didn't need to ask, but his imagination might make things far worse than they really were.

"It's bad, I won't lie. According to our source, we haven't been able to find her because she'd been held captive for all these weeks after her cover was blown. Garcia's had her this whole time, and who knows how he tortured her or what intel she gave them because of it. Training to resist is one thing, but enduring the kind of torture Garcia inflicts is another." Vance released a long breath.

Brent imagined getting his hands on Garcia. He couldn't wait for that moment. He wanted to bring the man down for what he'd done to Carmen, for what he'd done to his own sister, Adriana. For what he planned to do if he ever got his hands on her.

Over my dead body.

Brent had a feeling it just might come to that.

They approached the village near the coast just before dawn.

"Let's make this quick, Colt. In and out before anyone's the wiser."

"Right. Garcia's men could know by now we've come across the border. We could get swallowed up by his horde if we're not careful."

Brent, who'd been driving the SUV for the last four hours, parked behind a building three blocks down from the house where Carmen had supposedly hidden. They hiked along the edge of the quiet street in the predawn hour, hoping they wouldn't draw attention.

They approached the small house, and Colt quietly knocked on the door. Brent shared a look with his partner on this mission. They'd held on to hope all this time, but it was fading.

Their weapons were out of sight, but both of them palmed the guns resting in their holsters. Brent slowly drew his.

Colt knocked again.

The door barely cracked open, but no one was there.

Brent nudged his partner to look lower. His gaze slid down to a smallish young child, her sleepy eyes innocent and unafraid. Brent squatted down to be eye level with the child.

"We're here for the woman," he said in Spanish.

The child's eyes grew wide. "Are you going to hurt her?"

The words injured Brent, and he shook his head, softened his expression and replied. "No, sweetheart, we want to help her. She's one of us. We're her friends."

That seemed to satisfy the child.

Then a woman's voice scolded the child from behind and the door slammed. And the woman bolted the door. Brent stood and knocked on the door, maybe too forcefully this time. "We're friends. Please let us in."

"Should we break it down?" Colt asked quietly.

Brent saw window blinds shifting in the

houses around them. They were being watched, which meant their time was running out.

"It would seem there's a woman here, and I hope it's Carmen, but let's give it another try." Just as Brent lifted his hand to knock, he heard the bolt unlatching and the door opened.

An elderly man eyed him.

Brent softened his expression, hoping he didn't look intimidating. They wanted these people to cooperate. "We heard our friend is here. We've come to take her home."

The man seemed to look right into Brent's soul, and whatever he saw there appeased him because he ushered Brent and Colt through the door quickly and quietly, then shut it behind him.

Brent started to introduce himself, but the man wouldn't have it. "No names."

The man led them to a small room off the back. Brent's heart ached at the sight that greeted him. He and Colt eased closer to the bedraggled bed. A dirty bandage wrapped the thin dark-haired woman's head. Her gaunt face was clean, at least.

"Carmen," Colt said softly.

When her eyes blinked open, she turned her head as though it hurt to do so and looked at them. Confusion poured from her gaze. Confusion and fear. She scooted back into the corner, as if to get away from them.

"It's me. It's Colt. And Brent. Don't you remember us?"

She shook her head and turned away from them to face the wall as though that action would protect her. She was much worse off than they had anticipated. Still, they were grateful to have found her alive. Colt gently took her hand, but she snatched it back.

Brent noted her fingernails had been removed and were slowly growing back. Garcia was a monster.

The elderly woman who'd closed the door in his face came into the room and apologized. She didn't want their granddaughter opening the door to strangers. The woman's expression turned kind now as she explained they'd found this woman on the beach unconscious and concluded that she must have fallen and hit her head.

Men from the cartel had been searching for a woman earlier in the week, and the old woman feared their guest was the one who had been hiding from them. They'd brought her home under the cover of darkness and had hidden her away, only sharing the news with their closest friends in the village, hoping word would get out to the right people such as the

Texas Rangers or someone who could take her somewhere safe. She reported that Carmen had remained disoriented and fearful since waking up only days ago.

"But you must hurry now," the woman added.

"If you have found her, others will soon find her," the elderly man explained.

"Thank you for taking her in and getting word to us. But what about your safety, if these others come here to look for her?" This elderly couple had risked their lives.

"We will deny it, of course," the woman said.

The man lifted the child into his arms. "No. We will do more. We will leave and head to the mountains to stay there with my cousin. We leave tonight."

The woman nodded her agreement before focusing on Brent again. "Now, go. You must hurry before the village is awake to see you. Most of them are good people and will protect you, but there are a few who cannot be trusted."

Brent nodded.

"I'll bring the vehicle closer," Colt said. "You meet me at the door with Carmen."

It was a smart plan. They'd have to carry her

out and that would definitely draw attention. The faster they could pull away, the better.

After Colt left, Brent gently took Carmen's hand. "Your name is Carmen. I'm Brent. I'm going to get you out of here and to safety. Will you trust me?"

Tears pooled in her eyes. He could tell that she wanted to believe him, but she was afraid to trust. *Lord, help her to see clearly. Help her to recognize me.* He couldn't wait long for her to come to her senses.

"I'm just going to lift you in my arms so I can get you into our vehicle. Is that okay with you?"

Slowly she nodded. "Br-Brent?"

He smiled. "That's right, Carmen. It's Brent. Colt and I are taking you home."

He slid his arms under her frail, damaged body and lifted her against him. Then he followed the elderly couple to the door.

The little girl clung to his leg. "Is she going to be okay?"

"Yes, she's going to be just fine."

Carmen let her head rest against Brent's chest. "I'm going back to Texas," she whispered.

In the vehicle, Carmen rested in the back seat as they raced through Mexico to the United States border. Brent could almost breathe a sigh of relief. *Almost.* But they were deep in the country where Garcia had a stronghold, and the closer they drew to the border, the more danger he sensed awaited them.

"One down and one to go," Colt said.

"Come again?" Brent asked.

"We have Carmen back. And thank You for that, Lord. Now we just need to take down Garcia."

"We need fresh intel."

"It's been silent out there regarding Garcia."

"Not like we haven't been engaging with his men, but we need to get him in the flesh."

Brent's cell rang. A call from the safe house where Adriana was staying. His heart hammered. He hadn't planned to go back there unless it was absolutely necessary. A call could mean she was in danger again.

"McCord speaking."

"Your girlfriend contacted Garcia."

Adriana paced the small room, shouting her displeasure in Spanish at being locked inside. Most of these Texas Rangers could understand her, but she wasn't so sure about the additional security detail they'd put on the house. She'd obviously lost their trust.

Maybe she should have waited to talk to Brent before she'd sent the email. She'd sneaked into one of the off-limits rooms and used one of the Ranger's laptops to contact her brother. It wasn't likely that his tech man could locate them here at the safe house quickly, but the Rangers were talking about another move to a new house.

The rules said she wasn't supposed to call out or email. She wasn't supposed to make any contact whatsoever, especially with her brother. And no one seemed interested in getting her explanation for why she'd broken that rule.

The door opened and in stepped Brent Mc-Cord, looking more haggard than she'd ever seen him.

"Why'd you do it?" he asked.

She wanted to rush to him and wrap her arms around him. Let him hold her, make her feel secure, wipe all her worries away. She wanted this man, the only one she could trust, to stay near and watch over her, but he'd been sent away. And now, looking at his expression, she saw that she couldn't run to him. The warmth and support she was used to seeing in his eyes had vanished completely. She'd ruined everything.

Hurt edged his voice. Distrust lurked behind his gaze and in his demeanor. "I asked why you did it. Why did you contact Garcia?"

Foolish girl she was, tears welled in her eyes. "For you, Brent. For us."

"Don't give me that. Have you been lying to me about everything?"

"How can you even say that? Think that?" She took a step forward, wanting to go to him.

He put his hand out warning her off. "Don't even."

"I tried to talk sense into one of your Rangers. I tried to explain that, to capture my brother, we need to lure him out with the promise of the location of the drugs. That's the only way to end this. Your team could spend years chasing him without any success. Years during which I'd have to stay in hiding. I won't do it. I won't live like this. But I couldn't convince the Ranger to even call your boss, Major Vance."

Brent studied her, weighing her words against what he wanted to believe and what he should believe. His trip to Mexico had changed him somehow. She wanted to know that story, but now wasn't the time to ask.

"So you just took matters into your own hands and contacted your brother?" His volume had increased with his outrage. "That's not how we operate around here. We don't contact heads of cartels to make a deal without thoroughly thinking it through. Don't you get it?"

"That's just it. I *have* thought it through. I will offer Rio what he wants more than he wants me—his drugs and the cash. And the Rangers can hide and wait for him to come and get them. Now, tell me that isn't a good plan."

"The problem is that you could have already given away this location. Do you know if he has the technology to track your email? No, scratch that. We can't take the chance. We're moving within the hour. And you're not to contact him again."

"No. Let me do this. Let me lure him in. You can take him down."

Brent turned to exit the door and she flung herself at him. "Brent!"

He stiffened as she wrapped her arms around his waist, pushed her forehead into his back. "Please…" she whispered.

Turning, he shifted and she thought he would push her away from him, but he drew her to him instead. "You know we can't do this, Adriana. You know we can't be together."

Despite his words, she felt comforted by his gentle touch. She pressed her face against his chest and nodded. "Yes, I know, but I was so worried about you going to Mexico. I was worried my brother would find you and use you against me if he found out…if he found out that I care for you. Did you find the Ranger you were looking for?"

"Yes."

"And?"

"She's alive, but she's been tortured. She's barely coherent right now and seems very confused. Who knows what she told them." A deep aching pain resounded in his tone. His body shuddered.

Adriana wanted to cry. "This is why we have to stop him now."

"I want… I want to stop him. I don't know how much longer I can do this. I want it to be over, the same as you."

She pushed away from him to look into his face—his handsome features rough and his eyes framed in dark circles. The man badly needed sleep, a shower and a shave, and still he was the handsomest man she'd ever seen. "Does that mean you'll let me try?"

He nodded. "I'll have to convince Vance."

"I can—"

"No. You've done enough damage already."

"Do you think you can convince him?"

"I'm not going to try. I'm going to convince Colt, who'll convince him. I think my credibility is long gone when it comes to you."

And that grin, that adorable grin. He wanted to kiss her, she could tell. But he released her and stepped back. They shared a silent look that said it all, and then he said, "I can't do this, Adriana. I care too much already."

FOURTEEN

Tomorrow would be New Year's Eve. Adriana could hardly believe how fast the week had gone by and how much had happened since Christmas, especially now that she'd been confined with nothing to do but wait things out. Today seemed to drag on. Waiting for the verdict, her nerves were on edge. She and Rosa had been separated after the Rangers discovered she'd contacted Rio. She figured they would be moving to a new house within the hour, like they had told her, but more than two had already gone by. Arrangements had to be made and that took time. Approval from the powers that be. Phone calls.

Everyone was not only fuming mad at her but frustrated with Brent. And she felt horrible, just horrible, for putting him in that position. But she'd needed someone to listen. How appropriate that the one person to listen and hear her had been Brent, the one she'd dared to trust.

Her heart broke at the thought of him. His words came back to her.

I can't do this, Adriana. I care too much already.

Why did they have to be so drawn to each other, only to have the reality of their situation stand between them?

Dropping the spoon, she stood and paced the room, so tired of being held in the secure and safe location. While it was supposed to be for her protection, the restriction made it feel more and more like a prison.

When the door creaked open and Brent stepped inside, she released a long breath. "Well?"

"We're good to go."

"We're leaving?"

Colt followed Brent inside the room.

"No," Brent said. "I mean we want you to make the call to your brother. But first, we need to plan it all out."

"Let's agree on the terms before you talk to him." Colt glanced at Brent. "We think we can have everyone in place within the next few hours, depending on where you've hidden the drugs and cash."

"Wait a minute. This isn't some ruse so you

can recover those from me with no intention of baiting my brother, is it? I want your word on that. I want it in writing." Like that would do her any good in any court of law in the world—but she'd feel better, seeing it put down in black and white.

Brent frowned. "We wouldn't lie to you, Adriana."

He had fallen back to calling her by her name instead of honey. For a short time, she'd let herself exist in that dream world where he was her man and she was actually someone close to him. Someone who deserved the endearment from him. But she couldn't hold on to that dream anymore. She was back in the real world now.

"Oh, yeah? Your men work undercover. You lie all the time."

Colt blew out a big breath. Eyed Brent.

"Only because it's necessary to do that to… get information," Brent said.

She arched a brow.

"It's not like our covert Rangers can walk into a drug cartel and join the ranks there as a Ranger. Of course we have to use cover stories." Brent paced. Ran his hand through his hair. "Look, Adriana. What do you want? Do you want to make the call without planning this out? Things could get out of hand. You could agree to something, some situation in which we can't protect you, can't be there to arrest Garcia. I need you to trust me. Will you do that?"

"To a point. I will reveal nothing until I've spoken to my brother and he's agreed to meet me. Then I will contact him again with the exact location. You will learn of it at the same time."

"No!" Colt yelled. "Talk some sense into her, will you, Brent?"

"It's my only leverage," she said. "I promise you're likely closer to where I've hidden the drugs and cash than he is."

Colt got in her face, his expression dead serious. "Make the call, get his agreement, then tell him to drive a certain distance, after which you will contact him again with the exact location. While he's waiting for the exact location, you can tell us and we can be there, hidden and ready and waiting. And you will be safely here until this is over, after which you will serve as a witness to his crimes at the trial. You'll stay in the WITSEC Program as long as necessary. Cooperating will ensure your freedom against obstruction charges and more. That's the only way this will work, Adriana. We have to be there first and in place before your brother has a chance to arrive. You have to be safe and serve as a witness. Or else the deal is off."

What? She glanced at Brent. She wanted to explode, to blow up at both of them. She felt betrayed. She'd trusted Brent, and by extension the Texas Rangers. She should have known. She had only tried to escape a cartel. Had only meant to bring it down and save lives. Their refusal to see that made her want to scream at them. But giving them that piece of her mind at this juncture wouldn't help her case or her cause. She drew in a breath to calm her nerves. "I never meant to put anyone in harm's way."

She looked to Brent for his reassurance, but he averted his gaze, then hung his head. He probably believed she'd betrayed him by contacting Rio.

Colt handed a burner phone over to her. "Do you know his number?"

"Yes…yes."

Her sweaty palm wrapped around the cell Colt offered. Heart pounding, pulse roaring in her ears, she tapped in the number that would connect her with Rio. She hadn't truly thought she would ever call this number, but the moment had come.

She hadn't yet hit the call button but simply stared at the number she'd punched in.

"You don't have to do this if you don't want to." Brent's voice was low and soft.

He meant well, but they both knew it was the only way. What was she supposed to do—live in a safe house forever? Watch the Texas Rangers be attacked and abused because of her as Rio searched for her?

No. "You know this is the only way," she said. She didn't look at Brent. She might lose her nerve.

Touching the call button, she watched the seconds count and waited for the connection. What if it went straight to voice mail? What would she say? Her throat grew dry and her knees shook. Colt led her to the chair at the table. He pressed the speakerphone button. Adriana shot him a glare, but before she could argue someone answered.

"Si."

It was him. Rio. She glanced at the two men in the room with her and gripped the table, clutching the edge.

"It's me." Adriana squeezed her eyes shut, terror coursing through her. Anger and fury rising to meet it.

Rio's next words weren't fit to be heard. But she endured them.

"Are you ready to listen?" she asked.

"I am not talking to you. You are with the Rangers."

"No, Rio, no. I'm…not. They have no reason to keep me." She glanced at the two Texas Rangers staring her down. Her heart felt cold and alone. She understood about deception sometimes being necessary when working with criminals, but she asked for God's forgiveness for her lies, all the same.

"Why are you calling me?" He ground out the words. "It had better be to tell me where I can find what you stole from me."

"Yes. That's why I'm calling. You can have it all, but I have a price."

"And what is that, little sister?"

Who was this man? Who was this person? It wasn't her brother. Since becoming the head of a cartel, he'd changed until she didn't recognize him anymore. Tears slipped down her cheeks. "I want the freedom to live without your interference. I want no part of the cartel. I want a future without fear that someone is coming for me to harm me or my friends. A life without having to look over my shoulder and be afraid. If you can give me that, promise me that, then I will return all that you are after to you."

"Not all, little sister. Not *all*. I want you, too."

"Then we don't have a deal." She started to end the call but hesitated.

"Wait," he said. "I'm a reasonable man. You aren't worth that much to me. I'm willing to forget you are my sister, that you ever existed, if you tell me where I can find what you took. Every last ounce, every last dollar had better be there."

"Then we have a deal, after all."

"On one more condition."

Her heart raced. "What?"

"You'd better be there. I want to look you in the face one last time before I set you free." She glanced at Brent. She had never planned to face her brother. Despite his words, she knew that Rio probably had no intention of setting her free. Like the undercover Rangers, he would lie to achieve his goals.

Brent shook his head and reached for the cell. She stepped away and out of reach. "No," he mouthed.

"I won't be there, brother. But you will have what you want and I will have my freedom."

"Then I will assume this is all a trap."

"No, Rio, please. Just take the money and your stupid drugs, and I'll even throw in the watch. Take all of that and leave me alone. Like you said, forget I ever existed."

"You will be there or I will not come. And if

I see anyone who even resembles law enforcement—police or Rangers or border agents—anyone even daring to look my way, I will leave without getting what belongs to me, because I, too, value my freedom. But I promise you, if that happens, I will never rest until I have you. Then I will make you watch while I torture your Ranger boyfriend—and then shoot him in the head."

The brutality of Rio Garcia's words rolled over Brent, shocking him with their intensity.

Adriana's eyes held his gaze. Tears glistened on her cheeks. "I will text you the exact location within the hour."

"No deal. I want the information now. Do not think you can fool me. You're playing with fire, Adriana. I will kill your boyfriend! And then I will kill your friends, one by one. But you I'll capture first—and I'll keep you alive to see all the suffering you've caused until you beg me to kill you."

Her knees nearly gave out and Brent quietly assisted her back to the chair at the table. Brent couldn't believe the venomous words Garcia spewed.

"This is what I will give you and no more," she said. "If I am to meet you there alone, then you, too, must be there alone. We will face each other for the last time. Just you and me. I will bring no one from law enforcement, and you will bring none of your men. Agreed?"

A second ticked by. Then two…

"Agreed," Garcia finally said.

Adriana sagged with her release of breath. Then she gave him instructions on where to head. "And while you are driving, I will text you the rest of the details. I'm willing to bend, to negotiate, Rio. Let's see if you can do it, too. Show me that you are the great business-man everyone says. We will meet one last time in this life. And the way you are going, my brother, I doubt I will see you in the next."

Garcia cursed.

Admiration for Adriana surged in Brent. Even though hundreds of miles stood between them, Rio Garcia was a terrifying force to be reckoned with, even over a cell phone. And yet Adriana stood up to him. The only prob-lem would be when she ended the call. They could not let her go and meet Garcia.

When it was over, she collapsed against the table.

Brent crouched next to her in the chair, lifted her chin. "Are you all right, honey?" He couldn't help himself. He'd meant to put a hard, cold wall between them, but at the sight of her distress, it disappeared like it had been nothing but smoke.

She barely lifted her chin for him.

"Okay, he's on his way, Adriana," Colt said. "Now, tell us where we can find the goods so we can be waiting for this brother of yours. We'll take him down, and then you'll have your life back."

She shook her head. "No. You—the Texas Rangers—will take my life then. You will bring me up on your charges and put me on your witness stand and I will never have my life back."

Brent took one of her hands in his. "Not for long. It won't last forever, just long enough to help us put him away, and then you are free to live your life."

Her warm brown eyes found him and what he saw there—the utter terror—nearly did him in. "What's wrong? What is it?"

"You know that's not true. Rio's henchmen will forever search for me. He will conduct his business from behind bars, if necessary. My only real chance to get away would be if I could actually trust Rio to give me my freedom, but I can't ever trust him."

Brent wasn't sure if he'd ever seen such complete hopelessness. He lifted her up from the chair into his arms. "Aw, honey. That's just not true. We can help you change your name and identity, and you can move far from the border and forget this life ever existed."

She burrowed her face into his shoulder as her own shook.

Colt's expression remained dire and serious. He gestured toward the woman in Brent's arms. "We need the location before it's too late."

"Now, Adriana, you have to tell us where to find the goods. You have to cooperate. I want that freedom for you just as much as you do. So tell us what we need to know."

"I can't."

"What?" Frustration built in his chest. He gripped her arms and put enough distance between them to look her in the eyes. "What do you mean, you can't?"

"I will not put you in harm's way. I will not send you or your Texas Ranger brothers to face off with my brother."

"You think we're going to let you go there to face him alone? You know he won't keep his word. He'll bring his men and he'll take you and then torture and kill you."

Adriana lifted her hands and ran them through his hair and down his cheeks. His stomach twisted into a tight knot. "I will not risk your life. Bad enough he's after me, but his vow to kill you... If something happened to you, I would always blame myself. I cannot work with you in this."

"Well, you're not going. You can't go alone, and you can't give the drugs to him. So, now you have him driving up the road to meet no one."

"I'm sorry. None of it has worked out like I wanted or hoped."

"Look." Colt approached them. "We're running out of time. You are now officially obstructing justice. You need to tell us where you have hidden the drugs and the money. Now."

Brent glared at Colt, his message clear. *Back off!* "Can you give us a minute, please?"

"You have three." Colt exited the room.

"We're not going into this intending to get hurt. We're going to capture and arrest your brother for his crimes and put him away. Don't you want that? You can't go alone. That's not even in the equation. And I promise you, even your brother doesn't believe for a second that you will. But we'll give him the impression that you have."

She blinked up at him, lines creasing between her brows. "What are you saying?"

Brent blew out a breath. If he'd learned anything about this beautiful, stubborn and determined woman, it was that she could negotiate with the best of them. She'd just negotiated with her brother without losing her nerve, and she had no intention of backing down against the Texas Rangers, either.

"I'm saying that nothing will be accomplished if no one goes. If the only way for us to get Garcia is for us to go together, then so be it. I'll be there close, but not where he can see me. The others will be too far for Garcia or his men to see, but close enough to act. I'm asking you to trust me, Adriana. I'll take them all down. I'll take down your brother *and* his henchmen." And now he was just blathering pure bravado.

A small smile lifted her lips. "It seems the only way for us to do this is together. We will either live together or we will die together."

FIFTEEN

Adriana never thought she'd be this vulnerable with anyone, but she knew her face revealed everything that was in her heart. Brent knew all of it now, and why shouldn't he? Considering they were both putting their lives on the line to end this.

"I never thought it would come to this," she said.

He leaned close, and she thought he might kiss her again. She inched toward him, wanting that kiss more than life itself at this moment, because it could very well be her last kiss. Her last moment alone with this man.

The door behind them opened. "Your time is up," Colt said. "Now, where have you hidden the goods?"

Brent stepped back, putting more distance between them. He nodded, reassurance in his gaze.

"I'm trusting you, Brent, to keep our agreement," she said.

"What agreement?" Colt said.

"She's giving us the information we want, but she's going," Brent said. "We're all going. I'll be close so I can take Garcia out. And the rest of you will be off-site, but close enough to act."

"What are you, crazy?"

"It's the only way, Colt. Enough. Time is wasting. Go ahead, honey, give us the coordinates."

"The llama ranch. Down a tunnel in the barn. Inez said the tunnel was there before she and her husband owned the ranch."

"What?" Colt paced the room. "This whole time you'd hidden the drugs, the cash, right there beneath our noses?"

Respect shone in Brent's eyes. "I figured."

"I need to text Rio the information."

"Not yet." Both Brent and Colt spoke at the same time.

"Not until he's closer. We don't want him calling in forces that might already be near the ranch. Let us get into position, then you can text him."

"But he's going to won—"

"Let him wonder, then. Let him sit in his vehicle and wait for your text. Let him fume. He wants that money and his product. He'll wait for it. You don't need to apologize. Right now you hold all the leverage. Remember that."

She had known that all along, in fact, and didn't need his reminder. But her brother terrified her, so maybe she did need to hear those words.

Brent ushered her out the door and into the SUV. Calls were made and orders were shouted. Guns and ammo and body armor were piled into vehicles.

"We're going to have to book it to get there today." Colt's tone left no doubt he was not pleased at her news. "Even if she does make him wait."

In the middle seat, Adriana watched out the window. While Colt drove, he and Brent talked strategy without her, but she absorbed it all.

What have I done?

They were going to die today. She just knew it.

The trees and farms and small towns raced by the window, and it was as if she were watching the last moments of her life pass her by. If she hadn't saved Brent that day, or maybe if she hadn't taken the watch, then she wouldn't be in this moment, traveling down the road at a high rate of speed to meet a man who had thought about nothing but finding and killing her for months.

But so many of the factors that had led her to this moment had been out of her hands. She had no control over the fact she'd been born into a family that eventually evolved into a cartel. And she'd wanted another life.

Brent reached over and gently squeezed her hand. He leaned closer. "Are you all right?"

She shook her head and turned to him. "No, I'm not."

His strong jaw twisted with the same pain she saw in his eyes. "You don't have to do this. You can go back. We can take it from here."

"I'm surprised that your Major Vance agreed to let me come at all. But I suppose getting Garcia is that important." *More important than my life, any one person's life.*

Brent might have thought he'd hidden that truth away, but she saw it plain in his eyes. She also saw that he didn't want to let her go, despite his earlier words of agreement to the plan.

"If it were up to me," he whispered, "I'd take you far away from here. Take you away from it all."

She laughed a little. "I don't believe you, but it's a nice sentiment."

"No, I mean it."

"What? That you'd give up your life and job

as a Texas Ranger for me? It's who you are, Brent. I wouldn't ask that of you."

Had she hurt him with her words? She reached up and palmed his cheek. This beautiful, rugged man had stolen her heart. Somehow she had to crush what she felt for him before it crushed her. They could never be together. And he was talking nonsense now. The fear he felt for what they were both about to face was getting to him.

"I need you to promise me something," she said.

"I will if I can."

"Focus on getting my brother. He's murdered so many people. Others have lived under his brutality for far too long. Get him and take him down. Don't think about protecting me. Because if you're too busy thinking about me and what we can't have together, you're more likely to fail us both."

"Truer words have never been said." Regret lodged in his gut. But he knew she was right.

And with those words, Brent focused his attention back on the road, though Colt was driving, until finally they stopped the SUV a few miles outside of the ranch and switched to another vehicle. Now Adriana would drive and Brent would remain hidden, hunkered down in the front seat as much as possible. Colt would take the SUV to meet the other Rangers near the back of the ranch. They were scheduled to get there ahead of Garcia, in case he suspected the ranch, but they couldn't be certain about anyone or anything. The intel they'd received via the two caretaker agents they'd put in place on the ranch after the explosion reported that they'd seen no sign of Garcia or his men.

If their intel was correct, then maybe they would have a real chance of pulling this off. But before they drove away, one thing remained.

Colt handed the cell phone over to Brent. "Don't text him until you're in position."

Brent watched Colt climb into the SUV, then just before he drove off, he gave Brent one last look and nodded—Brent understood his silent message. *Be safe, my brother.*

The next part of their plan was now in play. He rested against the seat and watched Adriana drive.

Unbelievably, she smiled. "You're not going to stare at me the whole drive, are you?"

"Maybe."

She swatted him with her right hand. "Come on, you're distracting me."

She hit a pothole that jarred him and laughed. "You did that on purpose."

"Maybe."

He chuckled. "Crazy that we're laughing." But it felt good.

"Well, maybe we need some levity to survive this. I won't lie to you, Brent. I'm scared."

"I know." *So am I.* "But we both believe we're doing the right thing, and this is the only way. And we have to trust in God. You know your Inez is praying for you."

"Don't kid yourself. She's praying for *you*! She believes God sent you as my protector. So she's putting all her prayer power behind keeping you safe to protect me." Adriana's soft laugh held her affection for the woman. "I'm turning onto the main road that leads to the house now."

Brent called Colt on his cell. "Anything?"

"The ranch is still clear. Across the river is clear. We're almost in position here. Once you get there, she can text him. And, Brent?"

"Yeah?"

"I'm sorry I had to be so hard on her."

"I know. You're just doing your job."

"Yeah, about that…my job, that is. I want to keep it and I want to keep working with you. Please be careful. I heard what she said about not thinking about her because it will distract you. She's right."

"I know that. You don't need to tell me. So get your own focus back. This is for keeps."

"Right. For keeps. I'm out." Colt ended the call.

"I'm pulling up to the house now," she said.

"Pull around back to the barn, close enough I can sneak out in case we missed it and some-one's watching."

"Where are you going to be hiding?"

"Inside the barn makes the most sense. Whatever happens, Adriana, don't let him lay a hand on you. I don't want him to use you to protect himself, do you understand?"

She nodded. He squeezed her hand again.

"You said you would meet him. Didn't mean you have to stand close. He'll expect you to be on your guard—probably won't even be sur-prised to see you're wearing a protective vest."

When the vehicle came to a stop, he handed the cell over. "You can text him now. We have Rangers and other agencies in place, but not close enough to scare off Garcia or any men he brings. Any sign of trouble, you run for cover. All we need is to get him here and out in the open so we can arrest him."

Brent watched her slender fingers type in her message to her brother. She stared at the cell and waited for a reply and got none.

He shrugged. "He'll be here. He's probably angry that you are playing games with him."

"He probably suspects something."

"He's willing to risk a battle with us to get his goods back." And Garcia was probably glad for an excuse to hunt Brent down and kill him. It was Adriana whom Brent was worried about.

He wanted to wish her well, and hug and kiss her again, but he had to stay focused. He nodded and she climbed from the vehicle. He slipped out the passenger door. Before he took off, she caught his attention.

He hesitated.

"Please make sure Kiana and Maria are not in the barn."

"Okay. I will. Now, don't talk anymore."

He sure hoped the llamas weren't inside, because that would complicate matters. But surely the caretaker agents had understood to clear the barn of the animals.

He sneaked into the barn and relief flooded him when he found it empty. He hiked up to the loft and located a window, along with a few cracks in the slats from which he could watch and shoot if necessary. If Garcia ended up in the barn, if he made it this far, then Brent would be here waiting to take him down.

Adriana leaned against the truck, hugging

herself. At least the weather had inched into the high fifties today, but if she had to stand there too long, she'd get cold. She turned around and looked at the barn as if searching for him.

Oh, no, honey don't do that. Don't look around for me. That's telegraphing that I'm here.

Fear for her gripped him.

How can I let her do this?

But there was no going back.

Maybe he wasn't the best marksman, the best man for this job, but he needed to be close because he wouldn't trust anyone else with her life. No, Brent had to be the one Ranger, the one law enforcement officer on the llama ranch close enough to protect her.

If gunfire erupted, the others would swarm the ranch and it would be over.

The only thing Brent wasn't sure of was who would walk out alive.

Father, please, protect us. I can't go through losing a woman who risked her life for me— the woman I'm in love with.

Why, oh, why had it come to this situation where he would fall for her? And she would have to be here to bait Garcia? He'd known, they'd all known all along, that Adriana was the key to Garcia. But he hadn't imagined that it would all come down to the absolutely worst scenario he could think of.

She pushed off the truck and came into the barn.

"I'm cold, sorry. Came inside to get warm."

"You could sit in the truck."

"I feel exposed out there."

He didn't blame her. "I'll let you know if I see—"

"What is it?"

He peered through his scope of his sniper rifle. "I see a plume of dust. Someone's coming."

"Oh, Brent. I don't know if I can face him." She paced back and forth.

"You wanted to do this. But I'm telling you that you don't have to."

"Okay. I won't. I'll just… I'll just wait here. Your men can get him anyway, right?"

"I hope so."

Brent kept peering through the scope.

"Is it him?"

"It's someone. He's alone. But I can't tell. I don't… I don't think it's your brother."

"What?" She climbed up the ladder and sat next to him. "Give me that."

Adriana peered through the scope. "It's not him."

Disappointment boiled in his gut. "It's a test. He's making sure you're here alone."

"And I'm not here. I'm not there, I mean. I'm a chicken. I made you bring me and I'm afraid."

The vehicle pulled halfway up the drive and stopped. Idled. The man got out and put his hands on his hips. Looked around. Called her name.

She flinched.

"What?" Brent asked.

"The voice. It sounded like Rio's."

The man got back into his vehicle and started backing up.

"He's leaving," he said.

"What? No, no, no." She climbed down the ladder and flew out the barn exit.

Brent wanted to snatch her back, but her sudden decision had caught him by surprise. He had no choice but to watch her from his hiding place at the barn window. She ran out in front of the truck and waved her arms.

The pickup stopped, then slowly moved forward. Stopped fifty yards away. The man got out again and moved to stand in front of the grille of his vehicle.

And Brent kept his rifle sights set on the man.

SIXTEEN

Had she made a mistake in thinking the man sounded like Rio?

"Where's Rio?" she called. "I agreed to meet only Rio!"

"Don't you recognize me, sister?" The man limped forward. His head had been shaved and tattoos covered every inch of visible skin. And something about his nose appeared different.

His drastically altered appearance punched her in the gut. "No, I don't recognize anything about you. The outside or the inside. You're not the same man I once knew. You're not my real brother. I only know your voice. I could never forget your voice." She hadn't been mistaken about that.

"Especially since you heard it mere hours ago. My promise to you remains. If you brought anyone with you, I will kill those you care about."

"What about you? You promised to come

alone. I will only show you what you want if you kept your promise."

"When did I make that promise?"

Moisture bloomed on her palms. Slicked down her back even in the cool winter day. Adriana had to remain strong on this day of all days. She could not let Rio see her complete and utter terror. "If you didn't keep your promise, then you will not see what you came for."

He took a step toward her. And then another one. "I will see it and more."

What should she do now? She wasn't clear on that. "I never thought the day would come when I would be looking my evil brother in the eyes again. If only you knew the grief that fills my heart. Look, just look at yourself, Rio. Look what growing up in a cartel family has done to you. Don't you remember when we were young and life was simple? You were such a happy boy who loved God. Who loved *Jesucristo*. I looked up to you, Rio. I looked up to you."

All these words she said as her brother continued walking toward her, and she continued backing up until she was against the vehicle she'd driven here. "And now you are nothing but a brutal, greedy killer."

Tears of grief and dread burned down her face. She shook, literally shook—no longer able to hide from him just how terrified she'd become. "Now go. Go get your drugs. Go get your money. It's all in the barn."

Where was Brent? She glanced over her shoulder. Oh, no. She'd done what Brent had warned against. She'd telegraphed his presence.

Rio tugged a weapon from his backside and fired at the barn. Adriana ducked, believing the shot had been meant for her, but he ran for her and snatched her up before she could flee. He pressed his weapon into her temple.

"Come out, come out, wherever you are, Ranger man. I knew I could trust my sister to bring you. She never had the strength, the drive, for the business. But she does have a weakness, and that's you, Brent McCord. Come out, or I'll kill her."

"No!" she screamed. "Brent, don't you dare!"

Rio pulled her hair, hurting her, but this time she wouldn't scream or cry out. She wouldn't let him feel her fear. "If you kill me, you have no leverage. None. They will kill you where you stand."

"Your life means something to them, sister. Unlike me. My life means nothing to them."

"You're wrong. If my life meant something to them, they would never have let me come here to see you."

"They had no choice."

Gunfire echoed behind them. What was happening? Had Rio's men already started engaging the Rangers?

Rio pulled her down with him against the truck. He pressed the gun under her chin. "My men are here with me. I have more than enough to take out your Rangers. So you will show me where to find what belongs to me now."

"Why should I?"

He spewed curses. Hit her over the head. Blackness edged her vision. Rio dragged her around between the truck and the barn. "Tell me!"

"The barn," she croaked. "In the barn. There's a hidden tunnel."

He grinned. "Let's go."

Rio pulled her behind him, waving his weapon around. Adriana was beyond glad they had made sure Kiana and Maria were safe and away from the barn.

Brent, where are you?

A man stepped out of the barn and joined Rio. It wasn't Brent. No, it was Hector Martinez—Rio's ruthless second in command. Rio had brought *Hector*? Her heart lurched.

Hector gestured up to the loft. "He's out cold."

"I'm taking him with me when we leave."

"No, Rio, no, you can't do this." Adriana

tried to pull away from him. She fought him. Smacked him in the face. Kicked him.

But then Hector grabbed her, held her arms down with his brute strength.

"If I get any more of this nonsense from you," Hector said, "I'm going to hurt you. Do you understand?"

She nodded, silenced by fear. She almost looked to her brother for protection from Hector. But he'd brought the man for a reason—to keep Rio from any weakness that might still remain for his own sister.

"Show me the tunnel," Rio demanded.

Adriana couldn't believe how completely their plans were failing. The other Rangers. Where were they? Still battling her brother's men? What was taking them so long? Were they truly outnumbered and outgunned by the Garcia cartel? Adriana's knees buckled. She could hardly stand. Her brother's most brutal lieutenant dragged her.

"Over behind the hay. You move it. There's a trapdoor beneath it to the tunnel."

Her brother grinned, revealing a couple of gold teeth. "You moved all that cash and the drugs yourself?"

She nodded.

"I would like to make you move it again and watch you do it. I would enjoy that very much, but I don't have the time or patience. I will wait and devise another form of punishment, some form of slavery in which you may serve me for the rest of your natural life."

"You agreed that if I gave you everything back you would let me go free."

He laughed. "I think we are beyond our agreements, don't you? You lied to me. You never meant to come alone. You meant to trap me, but you have always underestimated me, sister. And now you find yourself in your own trap that will bring you all the way home."

"I would rather die than go back to Mexico with you." Adriana spat at him, wondering where her defiance had come from. She let that rage drive her, infuse her.

She found her footing and moved the hay herself. "There. See the door. Go down and get your drugs yourself. I'm not going anywhere with you. Get your stuff and leave me alone."

Rio opened the trapdoor and descended the ladder. Hector seized her again and forced Adriana down into the dead-end tunnel, where she led Rio deeper into the passageway. When Inez had first shown this to Adriana, it had given her the idea to create smaller hiding places around the property. But this…this she could never have dug out herself. And it had been the perfect storage place. The perfect hiding place. It had taken her several trips and more strength and stamina than she'd known she possessed to transfer the Garcia cartel stash here—a risky and dangerous operation. But at the time, anger and a drive to make the world a better place had fueled her. Rio must have been furious once he realized, too late, that Adriana had been bold enough to steal from him.

She pulled a string and a light came on.

At first her brother glowed with excitement. Acted out like some sort of megalomaniac.

Oh, Jesucristo...

Her heart broke for his lost soul.

When Hector yanked her deeper into the tunnel, the reality of her situation quickly wiped away whatever momentary compassion she'd felt for her brother. Rio pulled her close and yelled into her face, furious at her for all the trouble she'd caused him. Forcing him to search for her and chase after her and now he'd have to move his stash to new storage, all while fighting off law enforcement. Then he smacked her, knocking her to the ground. She thought he enjoyed it too much.

A noise outside the tunnel drew Rio's attention. He sent Hector up the ladder to check it out.

Now was her chance. She'd already tried

talking, tried reasoning, though she'd known it would be a lost cause. Still, she'd had to try. Her escape was in her hands alone. She stayed low to the ground, acting as if she was still stunned from his abuse. If he reached for her, she would hit him where it hurt most and go for the gun.

But when he snatched her up as she'd expected he would, the muzzle of his gun was pressed into her temple before she could react. He dragged her to her feet and she saw Brent at the bottom of the ladder, pointing his own weapon.

He was too late to save her. To save them.

Why did I let her come?

Despite her "deal" with Garcia, their agreement about this meeting, Brent had known in his gut that her brother wouldn't keep his end of it. He wouldn't let her go free but would kill her anyway. Though Garcia likely wanted to take her alive so that he could make her suffer first. It was the only thing that had kept her alive this long. Why? Why did families do this to each other? Destroy each other this way? He shoved aside thoughts of his father's betrayal, the man his father had murdered— his own brother! Brent's uncle.

And focused on making the kill shot.

Garcia was no fool, and he positioned himself behind his sister, using her as a shield.

"Put your weapon down, Ranger, or I will kill her."

"You'd kill your own sister?"

"She is no longer my sister. My sister no longer exists."

"You kill her and you're dead, too. Because I'll shoot you. You have no way out of this."

Garcia laughed. He sounded crazy. "What are you proposing, Ranger? That I surrender? You're loco."

"How about we make a trade. You take me, instead."

"No!" Adriana cried.

Voices resounded above them and not the voices Brent wanted to hear. He was running out of time. Garcia grinned, knowing the end was near for Brent, as well.

It was now or never. He was risking both their lives. But the way he saw their situation, it was the best chance they had. He took aim and fired, the bullet hitting Garcia's arm. Garcia's weapon went off but missed Adriana's head by inches. Brent scrambled forward and tackled Garcia to the ground and pinned him there. The man writhed in pain. Adriana grabbed Garcia's gun and pointed it at him to free Brent.

Garcia's men came down the ladder and Brent picked them off one by one.

"What do you want us to do?" someone yelled down at Garcia. "We could smoke them out. Get a fire started."

"No! You idiot! That would burn up the drugs and money even if it didn't kill me, too," Garcia shouted in Spanish.

The man valued his life above everything else, no doubt there, and Brent would use that to the fullest.

"Tell them to back off or you're dead," Brent said. "Tell them to put their weapons down and back out of the barn or you're dead. We're coming out, but if they try anything…"

"I get it—I'm dead."

"And then what?" Adriana whispered.

He gave her a warning look. He didn't need her complicating his plans by asking questions.

But her fears reflected his own—had all his backup been taken out? Where were they? If they were alive and well, they should already have taken control of the ranch and this barn. But Brent couldn't think about that. He had to focus completely on getting them out of this.

Sweat trickled down his back. He noticed sweat beaded on Garcia's forehead, as well. Was the man finally realizing that the next few minutes would be his last? Or would his arrogance carry through to the end?

Garcia yelled to his men in Spanish, warning them to back off. Anyone who remained in the barn would answer to him. As if—the man acted like he would get out of this eventually. Not on Brent's watch.

He had him, and he wasn't going to let him go.

Getting up the ladder would be tricky.

To Adriana he said, "Stay close behind me. You understand?"

She nodded. "How are we going to make it out of this?"

"Trust, Adriana. Remember, we have to trust God with our lives." And hope the good Lord saw fit to deliver the other Texas Rangers to this barn in time.

Brent cuffed Garcia to limit his movement, but in front, or he couldn't climb the ladder. "Will you tourniquet his arm?"

Adriana complied. Tore part of Garcia's shirt and wrapped it around his arm. When she pulled it tight enough to slow the bleeding, her brother growled in pain. She and Brent received curses the entire time for their efforts.

The biggest risk was their next move. Getting the man up the ladder. If Garcia went first, he could use his higher position on the ladder to try to kick Brent in the face. If Brent went first and any of Garcia's men were still in the barn, he could be shot and killed. Still, he edged his way up slowly.

"Ask them if anyone remains."

"No." Garcia spat.

Brent descended the ladder and pointed the weapon at him. "Do it or it's over for you now."

"You can't kill me. I'm in handcuffs. You're a Texas Ranger. That's not how you operate."

"No, but I can." Adriana tightened her grip on Garcia's weapon. "And desperate times call for desperate measures. Do it, Rio. I might not kill you, but I will hurt you."

Something about the fire in her eyes and tone rang true for the man because he quickly spouted off his demands.

When no one answered, Brent assumed that meant Garcia's men were too far away from the barn to hear their boss shouting up from this tunnel. He'd told them to leave earlier—and they wouldn't dare disobey. So now it was time to move.

"I'm going first," Brent said. "Garcia comes after me. If he tries anything, shoot him."

She nodded. Brent smiled at her. Though these were dire circumstances with little to smile about, he couldn't help but admire her strength.

Even in the barn, they were essentially trapped unless the Rangers showed up. But then gunfire erupted outside the barn.

The Texas Rangers!

Except their appearance forced Garcia's men back into the barn, where they started shooting both to defend themselves from the law enforcement presence outside and to retrieve their leader. As Brent scrambled for cover with his prisoner, a bullet hit Adriana behind him and she fell. Likely her vest protected her, but she would be an easy target lying there, and there was too much that the vest didn't cover. Seizing the moment of distraction, Garcia head-butted Brent and ran, his limp slowing him. Brent fired at Garcia at the same time he crawled to Adriana to cover her.

Two of Garcia's men flanked him and they escaped the barn.

"Are you okay?"

Adriana blinked up at him and sucked in a breath. "It hurts, but yes. The body armor protected me."

"Then let's get you back into the tunnel until this is over. You have a gun." She nodded. He led her over and she crawled down.

"Aren't you coming?" she called up.

"I'm going after your brother."

And without another word, Brent turned

away from her before looking into her beautiful eyes clouded his judgment. He had to leave her there. That was his only choice. He couldn't let Garcia get away yet again.

Brent would end this today.

The cartel members had fled the barn with Garcia to protect him, and outside, the battle raged between Garcia's men and the Texas Rangers as well as additional LEOs.

Scanning the chaos, Brent finally spotted the drug lord. Flanked by two of his men, Garcia headed for his vehicle, stopping to take cover along the way. Brent did the same as he pursued Garcia in the midst of the battle. When the two henchmen turned and fired on him, he took aim and shot them both down.

Only Garcia was left and he turned to face Brent, backing toward his car.

"You're still in cuffs. You can't drive. You're not getting away this time." Brent marched toward the man.

Garcia exploded with fury and ran toward Brent. Brent stood his ground but didn't raise his gun. Garcia wasn't armed and Brent wouldn't shoot an unarmed man. Garcia rammed into him, knocking him to the ground. But both Brent's hands were free and he pounded the man in the face and head, knocking him out cold.

The next thing he knew Colt stood over him. "You okay?"

"Yeah. I got this."

Colt extended his hand and pulled Brent to his feet. "Sorry we got delayed. We had a small army to fight. Some of them are dead. Some ran away and some we caught. Glad to see that includes Garcia, thanks to you. Where's Adriana?"

"I left her in—"

"I'm here." Adriana stepped forward and pressed herself into Brent's arms. He had no choice but to wrap them around her—and there was nothing he wanted more.

No point in denying what he'd felt for her since the first moment he'd met her. But he had questions—could he trust anyone enough to truly love them? Was he good enough for her?

Garcia roused from his beating and was pulled to his feet. His eyes never strayed from Adriana.

"You're going away, Rio. You're going to spend the rest of your life inside a prison for your crimes and your murders. I truly hope you find yourself again while there. That you find *Jesucristo*," she said.

He spat at her. "I am making a vow here before you and your Ranger boyfriend. I vow to kill you. It doesn't matter if I'm in prison, my reach will remain outside the walls."

Brent wanted to respond, but there could be truth to Rio's words. "Come on." He pulled Adriana away from her enraged brother and headed back to the vehicle they had driven to the ranch.

He kept his arm firmly around her shoulders in case she wanted to turn back and try to reach out to her brother again. He wouldn't have it. "It's over."

Adriana shrugged away from him. "It will never be over."

Brent led her back to an overwhelmed EMT positioned by the ambulances. She was likely bruised from the gunshot to her chest. But she was alive. If only Garcia's threats didn't still hang in the air between them. The EMTs were busy attending to serious injuries, and unfortunately, Adriana would have to wait. Brent took the opportunity to turn her to face him.

"Don't worry about his threats, honey."

She angled her head up at him, relief and hope visible in her gaze…mingled with fear. She still wasn't free—they both knew it. Had they ever really thought she would be?

And as for things being over, really over—

that would mean that Brent would no longer have a reason to be in her life. He wasn't sure he liked that. In fact, he was positive he didn't.

"I… I thought I would feel free when this ended. But it will never end. What happens next?"

"You and Rosa are both witnesses to his crimes and will need to go into WITSEC until the trial."

"And what about after the trial? Like he said, he can control his people from inside the prison walls. You know this is true."

Unfortunately, he did.

He placed his hands on her arms and rubbed them to chase the chill away. And to connect with her. He had words to say, and frankly, they terrified him.

"What is it?" she asked.

If he didn't do this now, he knew he would never get another chance. Brent cleared his throat. "I don't want to lose you. Not when I only just found you again. Adriana, I think I have loved you from the first moment I saw you two years ago. Because I haven't stopped thinking about you. Spending these last few days with you only confirmed that for me, and I know I want you in my life."

Her expression grew somber. Uh-oh. Maybe

he'd taken things too far, and she didn't feel the same way.

"What exactly are you saying, Ranger Mc-Cord?"

And she'd referred to him by his formal title. Brent pursed his lips and tried to gulp air. He hung his head. How did he continue? He was making a fool of himself. Had he really thought she loved him, too?

She urged his face back up and then he saw her beautiful smile. "I feel the same way in case you were wondering."

That encouraged him to continue. He grabbed her up in his arms and gently kissed her. Man, it felt good to finally let himself love her. When he ended the kiss, he put her back on her feet.

His heart pounded. "Will you be my wife?"

Her eyes widened. "You'd do that? You'd marry the sister of a drug lord?"

"I want to marry the woman I love, and that's you."

"Then my answer is that I want to marry the man I love, and that's you, Ranger McCord."

EPILOGUE

New Year's Day, one year later

"I do," Adriana said as she gazed into the eyes of her cowboy protector, Texas Ranger Brent McCord.

Then the pastor pronounced them man and wife.

Only, she wouldn't remain Mrs. Brent Mc-Cord for long. No. Brent was leaving the Texas Rangers to enter the WITSEC—witness protection program—with Adriana, and they would have new names and a whole new life far away from the Mexican border. And Rosa would come along as her sister.

Brent leaned forward and kissed her gently, making her heart leap for joy—this moment had been so long in coming. He took her hand and together they turned to face their friends who had come to this small private wedding at yet another safe house. Adriana had been in protective custody through the trial until this moment when she would go with her new husband into WITSEC. If she'd gone into WITSEC earlier, she would never have been allowed to see him, so she'd opted to remain at a safe house throughout the trial.

She'd gotten to know Brent's Texas Rangers team members, too, over the course of the year, and now it would be so hard to say goodbye to her new friends, starting with Texas Ranger Austin Rivers and his bride, Kylie, and their precious baby girl, Mercedes. Oh, did that make her want a baby of her own. She just knew Brent would make the most amazing father.

And then there was Ranger Colt Blackthorn and Adriana's look-alike, Danielle. They decided they could have been twins!

Adriana had grown especially close to Ranger Carmen Alvarez, who, after her recovery, had insisted on being one of the Rangers who protected Adriana until the trial was over and Adriana and Brent would go with the US Marshals to their new life—today, actually.

Brent's boss on the team, Major Vance, shook Brent's hand and wished him well and kissed Adriana on both cheeks like she was a beloved daughter. And, of course, Christopher,

Trevor, Ethan and Ford were there, Ethan the only one of the four who had finally married.

Adriana had gotten to know their administrative assistant, Lizzie, and Jenny Fielding, the tech support person—all of the Rangers on the reconnaissance team.

They appreciated Adriana, because she had helped them complete one of their biggest tasks—the Garcia Mission. And in turn, they had helped to free her from her brother and build a new life for herself.

Inez stood just beyond the group of Rangers. Adriana pressed through them in the small room and went to the woman. Drew her into a hug. Inez would not be going into WITSEC with them but had sold the ranch and had moved in with her sister in Eureka, California. Adriana was grateful she'd been able to attend the small, secret wedding.

"I will miss you, Inez. I owe you so much. You saved me. You changed my life."

"Oh, sweet child, it does my heart good to know the Lord used me in such a way. All I ever wanted was to make a difference in even one person's life. I'm grateful to Him. God is good! And look—He has given you a whole new life with your Ranger man. I cannot even believe how well this has all turned out."

Adriana nodded. "I couldn't imagine that in

a little over a year, after running for my life and ending up at your ranch, I would be in this room getting married—to a lawman, no less!"

They laughed together.

The only thing her wedding was missing was her biological family. Though her brother was behind bars where he should be, and her testimony had helped to put him there, Adriana couldn't help the grief that tried to flood her at the chasm between her and the brother she used to love so dearly. But she pushed it back down. This scenario was as it should be. Things had been made right. Rio had made his choices long ago, and Adriana had been given a chance to be free to live her life. This was a joyous day, the most joyous she'd ever experienced, so she set any depressing thoughts about Rio aside and smiled again.

An arm slipped around her waist. She turned to see Brent smiling down at her, nothing but the purest joy mingled with love for her in his gaze. It made her knees weak.

"There you are," he said.

She laughed. "Like you would lose me in this room. It's so small."

"But it's filled with people."

"I know. It's filled with your closest friends." Adriana reached up and pressed her hands against his handsome cheeks. "And you're giving them up for me, Brent. Are you… Are you sure?" Her heart ached to have to ask the question, but she needed to know for certain.

He grabbed her hands and grinned—that grin she loved and could spend the rest of her life enjoying. "We've been over this already, honey. Don't worry. What would be the point staying with them if all I do is think about you all the time?" He lowered his voice to a whisper. "Besides, we're married now."

Brent scooped her up and close for a thorough kiss, then, "I love you."

Those around them started clapping and shouting, Texas style.

* * * * *

If you enjoyed
TEXAS CHRISTMAS DEFENDER,
be sure to get the first two books in the
TEXAS RANGER HOLIDAY *series.*

THANKSGIVING PROTECTOR
by Sharon Dunn
CHRISTMAS DOUBLE CROSS
by Jodie Bailey

Find more great reads at
www.LoveInspired.com.

Dear Reader,

What a wild ride this story was to write! I hope you enjoyed *Texas Christmas Defender*. I'm a seventh-generation Texan on both sides of my family and was once a member of the DRT—Daughters of the Republic of Texas. (I haven't paid my dues, so I can't say I'm still a member, even though my family has been in Texas long enough. Ha!) All this Texas family history and this will be my first book set in Texas. Can you believe it? I'm so happy I was given the opportunity to join this continuity series. The men and woman of the Texas Rangers have a rich heritage that begins early in Texas history and are world-renowned, often compared to Scotland Yard or the FBI. This is a *state* law enforcement agency, folks.

In *Texas Christmas Defender*, Adriana is looking for a refuge from some seriously bad people. Though escape nearly costs her everything—her safety, her life and the lives of those she loves—freedom from the evil that surrounds her is worth the cost. Inez is there to encourage her and pray for her. Isn't that just like how God works in our lives? He sends someone to us who can pray for us and nurture us in His ways. Even if we don't realize that person is there—trust me, they are. It's my prayer for you today that you turn to the only One who can give you a true safe haven. Who can be your true refuge.

Thank you for reading my books! To find out about my other books, visit my website at ElizabethGoddard.com!

Many blessings,
Elizabeth Goddard

Get 2 Free Books,
Plus 2 Free Gifts—
just for trying the Reader Service!

YES! Please send me 2 FREE Love Inspired® Romance novels and my 2 FREE mystery gifts (gifts are worth about $10 retail). After receiving them, if I don't wish to receive any more books, I can return the shipping statement marked "cancel." If I don't cancel, I will receive 6 brand-new novels every month and be billed just $5.24 for the regular-print edition or $5.74 each for the larger-print edition in the U.S., or $5.74 each for the regular-print edition or $6.24 each for the larger-print edition in Canada. That's a saving of at least 13% off the cover price. It's quite a bargain! Shipping and handling is just 50¢ per book in the U.S. and 75¢ per book in Canada.* I understand that accepting the 2 free books and gifts places me under no obligation to buy anything. I can always return a shipment and cancel at any time. The free books and gifts are mine to keep no matter what I decide.

Please check one:
☐ Love Inspired Romance Regular-Print
  (105/305 IDN GLWW)

☐ Love Inspired Romance Larger-Print
  (122/322 IDN GLWW)

Name _____ (PLEASE PRINT)

Address _____ Apt. #

City _____ State/Province _____ Zip/Postal Code

Signature (if under 18, a parent or guardian must sign)

Mail to the **Reader Service:**
IN U.S.A.: P.O. Box 1341, Buffalo, NY 14240-8531
IN CANADA: P.O. Box 603, Fort Erie, Ontario L2A 5X3

Want to try two free books from another line?
Call 1-800-873-8635 today or visit www.ReaderService.com.

*Terms and prices subject to change without notice. Prices do not include applicable taxes. Sales tax applicable in N.Y. Canadian residents will be charged applicable taxes. Offer not valid in Quebec. This offer is limited to one order per household. Books received may not be as shown. Not valid for current subscribers to Love Inspired Romance books. All orders subject to approval. Credit or debit balances in a customer's account(s) may be offset by any other outstanding balance owed by or to the customer. Please allow 4 to 6 weeks for delivery. Offer available while quantities last.

Your Privacy—The Reader Service is committed to protecting your privacy. Our Privacy Policy is available online at www.ReaderService.com or upon request from the Reader Service.

We make a portion of our mailing list available to reputable third parties that offer products we believe may interest you. If you prefer that we not exchange your name with third parties, or if you wish to clarify or modify your communication preferences, please visit us at www.ReaderService.com/consumerchoice or write to us at Reader Service Preference Service, P.O. Box 9062, Buffalo, NY 14240-9062. Include your complete name and address.

LI17R2

Get 2 Free Books,